Special Agent Hunter

SPECIAL AGENT HUNTER

Single Title Series Book #10

Mimi Barbour

Sarna Publishing

Contents

Contact Me
308

Dedication

I wanted to make this a dedication to the beginning of 2021.

This last year has been a terrible time for so many... no matter where you live. The pandemic has touched all of us in various ways – none of them positive. Now with the coming vaccines, we can see a light, move on, and rebuild our lives.

I pray in the future, we'll be able to read an entertaining story and lose ourselves in an enjoyable experience without having to eventually face black times at the end of the make-believe world.

I envision all who've suffered, who've lost loved ones, and send my love.

Mimi

Praise

Reviews for Special Agent Hunter.

"Another great story and characters told by a wonderful story teller. I was drawn into the story from the start and had trouble putting the book down until I was finished. I try to summarize the story and find myself rewriting the whole story. If you have read other books by Ms Barbour you will not want to miss this one. If you haven't read any of her books this is a good place to start." ~reviewed by Janine

"Once again you've written another terrific "Undercover FBI" book! I was so excited when I found out "Special Agent Sophie" was not the last! Cora is an amazing heroine, from beginning her career as barely a year in rookie scared to take a kill shot for protection of citizens of New Orleans and wherever next the serial killer was going, to a take no names, but caring, hard axx Detective who worked saving, getting who she could, and never giving up!

Add a terrific OCD hero, Special Agent Kal Hunter who was there in the beginning and clearly sees an entirely different woman, and you have an amazing novel of growth, suspense, and definitely some of your terrific one-liners that will crack readers up.

I loved the full circle theme, the rookie, Cora, that Special Agent Kal tried to have removed from the force because of her inability to do what he thought was best.

Sam and Bonny, wow, Sam a canine who adopted Kal, regardless of Kal's feelings about the matter, was an amazing secondary character. Sam seems K-9 trained and seems so very human. He even insists harshly that the puppy, Bonny becomes part of Cora's family.

Now without giving away the story, you gave some minor clues that really got me, but until almost the end, I was surprised. It ended so well.

Especially love Kal's last line to Cora. Happy, but definitely ended on a terrific laugh.

Another fun, suspenseful, (yep they can go together) strong heroine and perfect matched hero story yet again, from Ms Barbour!

Loved!

Sooooooo ...

Again ...

NEXT ... !!!!!!!! ?" ~ reviewed by Karen

~~~~~~~~~~~~~~~~~~

"Love Mimi Barbour, love her books. When you can read a book that within just a few words, you are brought right into the book. You feel, taste, see everything going on. Great story lines. Fantastic characters, fantastic plots, story lines like real life both honest folk and of crooks. Humor that will have you giggling then full on belly laugh. You may even shed a tear or two." ~ **reviewed by Shirleen Miller**

"As a writer myself, I think that one of the true marks of an excellent author is solid, believable character development, and in my opinion, Mimi Barbour is the master of character development!" ~ **reviewed by author Flo Barnett**

Also author of...

Love Me Tender (Book 2)
Don't Be Cruel (Book 3 – to be released spring
of 2021)

***

Vegas Series
— Action–Packed Thrillers! —
Vegas Series – Complete Boxed Set
Partners (Book 1)
Roll the Dice (Book 2)
Vegas Shuffle (Book 3)
High Stakes Gamble (Book 4)
Spin the Wheel (Book 5)
Let it Ride (Book 6)

***

Undercover FBI Series
— Popular & Compelling! —
Special Agent Francesca (Book 1)
Special Agent Finnegan (Book 2)
Special Agent Maximilian (Book 3)
Special Agent Kandice (Book 4)
Special Agent Booker (Book 5)
Special Agent Charli (Book 6)
Special Agent Rylee (Book 7)
Special Agent Murphy (Book 8)
Special Agent Sophia (Book 9)
Special Agent Hunter (Book 10)
Special Agent Makayla (Book 11 – to be released
spring of 2021)

***

Holiday Heartwarmers Series

— Truly a Christmas favorite! —
Holiday Heartwarmers Trilogy
Please Keep Me (Book 1)
Snow Pup (Book 2)
Find Me a Home (Book 3)
Frosty the Snowman (Book 4)
Love of my Life (Book 5)
A Perfect Storm (Book 6)
Alone at Christmas (Book 7)
***

Her Sweet Revenge Series
— She's unstoppable! —
Retaliation (Book #1) FREE
Justice (Book #2)
Resolution (Book #3
Endings – (Book #4)
Faith (Book #5)
Leni (Book #6)
~*~*~

Single Title Series
He's My Baby (Book #1)
Christmas Runaway (Book #2)
Because You Cared (Book #3)
Daddy's Mine (Book #4)
Her Hero (Book #5)
You Make Me Happy (Book #6)
Sweet Christmas (Book #7)
You're the Boss (Book 8)
***

The Best in Romance Series

Red Hot Divas (Book #1 Box Set)
Hot and Handsome (Book #2 Box Set

~*~*~*~

Other Titles
I'm No Angel
Hotshot Cowboy
Big Girls Don't Cry
The Surrogate's Secret
Mimi's Mix (Box Set)
'Tis the Season (Box Set)
Hearts, Flowers & Romance (Box Set)
Love, Christmas (Multi-author Box Set)
Unforgettable Romances (Multi-author Box
Set)
Sweet and Sassy (Multi-author Box Set)
Unforgettable Heroes (Multi-author Box Set)
Unforgettable Christmas (Multi-author Box
Set)
A Christmas She'll Remember (Multi-author
Box Set)
Unforgettable Valentine (Multi-author Box Set)
A Valentine She'll Remember (Multi-author
Box Set)
Unforgettable Suspense (Multi-author Box Set)
Unforgettable Danger (Multi-author Box Set)
Unforgettable Trouble (Multi-author Box Set)
Unforgettable Weddings (Multi-author Box
Set)
A Wedding She'll Remember (Multi-author
Box Set)

Sweet and Sassy Brides (Multi-author Box Set)
Love, Christmas 2 (Multi-author Box Set)
Sweet and Sassy Suspense (Multi-author Box Set)
Unforgettable Thrills (Multi-author Box Set)
Unforgettable Passion (Multi-author Box Set)
A Romance She'll Remember (Multi-author Box Set)
Sweet and Sassy Cinderella (Multi-author Box Set)
Unforgettable Power (Multi-author Box Set)
Daring Protectors (Multi-author Box Set)
Unforgettable Charmers (Multi-author Box Set)
Sweet and Sassy Baby Love (Multi-author Box Set)
Sweet and Sassy Heroes (Multi-author Box Set)
Unforgettable Intrigue (Multi-author Box Set)
Unforgettable Christmas Dreams (Multi-author Box Set)
Sweet and Sassy Holiday (Multi-author Box Set)
Christmas Shorts (Multi-author Box Set)
Unforgettable Temptations (Multi-author Box Set)
Unforgettable Surrender (Multi-author Box Set)
Unforgettable Deceptions (Multi-author Box Set)
Unforgettable Joy (Multi-author Box Set)
Unforgettable Sweethearts (Multi-author Box

Set)
Unforgettable Christmas Joy (Multi-author Box Set)
Dear Santa – A Christmas Wish (Multi-author Box Set)
New Year's Eve Shorts (Multi-author Box Set)
Unforgettable Revenge (Multi-author Box Set)

***

All Mimi's books can be found on her Amazon Author Page:
http://bit.ly/MimiBarbourAmazon
OR
Website: http://mimibarbour.com

Chapter One

June 1st

Another murder?

Jesus, the ten-year-old, cold-case killer had struck again. Because the first murder seemed highly unlikely to have been done by the same person, Special Agent Kal Hunter had written it off as a circumstantial improbability. But this new evidence stared him in the face and couldn't be ignored.

The report of the recent killing had arrived in his inbox just as he'd decided to call it a day. Of course, it messed with his idea of closing up shop and heading to the bar before the summer sunset at nine p.m. or thereabouts.

Considering the clock had struck that hour a few minutes ago, it appeared tonight would be like all the others, with him still at his desk till the late

3

hours.

Accepting the inevitable workaholic nickname, he began listing the very reasons these murders had rung his memory bell so loud that he'd contacted some old NYPD cohorts, and got through to the Cold Case Unit.

They'd implemented a database to track unsolved homicides and to digitize cold case files for the preservation of documents and evidence over time.

Back then, when the murders had gone down, he'd been wearing the NYPD police badge, and he remembered the overall circumstances, just not the particulars.

Shawn Bonaire, his old partner, would have been able to remind him of the facts without him having to check, but the bastard had retired early. Both had memorized this case mainly because they'd rehashed it for years and had finally been forced to give up. The killer had gotten away with his crimes, and that fact had rankled Shawn for a lot longer than it had eaten at Kal.

Of course, the difference in their ages might have been a factor. Since he'd been almost twenty years younger than the man he'd aspired to become, he accepted the life his partner wanted and kept his mouth shut about having to work without him.

Kal flopped back in his chair and began rearranging the numerous files he'd printed out.

Surprised that they seemed out of order to the way he'd have arranged them, he shook off his OCD and continued to place them on his desk, putting the murders back in the order that they happened.

As if he sensed the recent promise for a walk had been canceled, his mutt, Sam, lying prone beside his desk, let out a begrudged whine before accepting the inevitable. His sad eyes filled with objections glared at Kal.

"I'm sorry, big boy, we'll go out soon, I promise." Kal reached down to stroke the huge animal in remorse. He still had trouble believing that he'd adopted the ugly thing after the animal had followed him home and refused to leave. Over the next two days, he'd come so close to calling SPCA, had even threatened to do so numerous times when the dog insisted on getting his own way but hadn't.

It still freaked him out that he'd never gone through with his multiple threats. How could he when he saw those big, saggy eyes gazing up at him? Never mind the lolling tongue that cleaned his face in one swoop when he stupidly got too close. He decided that a German Shephard must have gotten involved with a Shar Pei, add a Malamute in the mix with blue eyes and that came close to describing his huge pet. He opened his drawer noticing Sam suddenly peer up at him with interest.

The dog knew that sound. It meant a chewy

bone and sure enough, Kal held one up as a treat. He fondled the now happy dog around his overly large right ear, the one that stood up properly, unlike the left ear that flopped over as if dead. One would think this comic appearance would make the animal look less threatening. Not true.

Kal pulled his attention back on the papers in front of him. *Yep, here's the list he'd made back then.* One of the killer's quirks jumped out at him.

Smearing the crime scene and wrecking all the signs that forensics might use as evidence, or to track the killer's habits, was itself an MO. That's what had red-flagged this ancient case after the first recent murder.

At the second current crime scene, the killer had left even more proof that he'd started playing those same games again. He'd switched his murder weapon in the exact way he'd done ten years earlier.

Victim number one came to his end from a point-blank gunshot to his heart. Number two had been stabbed with an ordinary, everyday hunting knife just like the newest gruesome act showed. Stabbed in the chest, close enough to the heart that it stopped beating in seconds. And again, the crime scene had been messed with, destroyed on purpose.

If the depraved maniac continued to play by the old rules, he'd be using a hypodermic needle thrust in the neck to end the third unfortunate's existence.

Not that he'd chosen to off average citizens whose families would grieve their loss this time around. Nope! He'd changed his tactics to kill the city's Most Wanted – yet not arrested – because of loopholes that every cop detested.

Again, it's like he knew the bad guys in and around his New York stomping grounds and had opted to rid the world of two of the most notorious assholes he'd decided shouldn't be allowed to live... vermin that every officer would love to put away for good.

Agent Hunter flopped back in his chair and covered his forehead with his clasped hands. The latest news had him sweating big-time. Just as he'd been involved in those earlier cases while working homicide, he had the old files spread over his desk and sunk into the same futility he had ten years ago. Back then, the murdering prick had been numerous steps ahead of them from the beginning.

He remembered his whole unit had been working overtime for weeks, trying to second-guess the animal to stop the spree of bodies that to this day, they'd found had no significant connections. It had been like the man with the hate-filled heart had decided at the spur of the moment, he'd take this or that life, and then did so.

Flipping to the last section of pages, he knew what to expect. The first bunch of killings had happened right here in the big city, but then the maniac had moved to another stomping ground. Those last multiple murders had taken place in New Orleans. His memory kicked in. Picking up that bunch of printouts, he read where the Deputy Chief of Police and his assistant had gotten close to capturing the suspect who they'd identified as male. Due to the incompetence of one woman, they'd failed dreadfully.

It had been that young patrol officer who'd froze and missed the only chance they'd had to put the bastard out of his misery. The one upswing on that thought had been that the killings had then stopped. His binge came to an end, and he hadn't killed again.

Near the back of the papers, he stumbled upon the image of the young female officer, tiny yet holding her back stiff while standing in the shadow of her boss. Female eyes, naked of any artifice, appeared huge in her white, bruised face. Her lips swollen from her battling the perp, the modest ponytail, everything screamed of her simple rookie looks that he'd not forgotten.

In fact, though he'd never admit it, she'd haunted his dreams for months after the incident. He hadn't forgotten the silent screams her eyes portrayed once she'd stumbled upon the bodies of the killer's last victims. Sympathy had surged inside him, but his frustrated anger had buried it.

Self-conceit emerged as if he would never... could never have made such an error. And she'd known his condemnation for what it appeared. A man disrespecting his peer, looking down his nose as if he had every right.

A chump having the audacity to disapprove rather than behaving in the way he would today. As a man with as many flaws as anyone else, one who'd suffered more times over foolish errors than he'd ever have thought possible, an idiot who'd never again think himself above his equals today. He'd disparaged her and had never had the opportunity to apologize.

Kal picked up the phone to make a call to the New Orleans police department and found that Captain Joe Mason had graduated from his post to now hold the position of Deputy Superintendent. He'd been replaced by the detective he'd worked with ten years earlier who was now the Captain for the 8th District. The very man who'd stayed in his mind periodically as a guy who stood up for that same young woman who should probably never have been a cop.

Seeing again those big, tear-filled eyes full of remorse before she'd run to the bushes and emptied her stomach, he flinched. Her unfired gun lay on the ground where she'd dropped it. Earlier, unlike others, she'd had the shot. In fact, the animal had all but begged her to take it, and she'd cringed and failed.

Because of her actions, later that night he'd killed his last victims, a family of four who hadn't deserved to die. Then he'd disappeared for good.

Kal still felt that anyone so unsuited to their responsibilities had to know the truth about herself and her abilities. Not having the instincts to shoot wasn't a bad thing, except when you're wearing the uniform, it's your responsibility, especially when it meant saving lives.

Hopefully, they'd taken his advice, and made her give up the badge she should never have worn. Truth be told, he didn't want to see her again. Brushing aside the familiar angst that had eaten at him for so long after those days, he picked up the files again.

Re-evaluating the ten-year-old itinerary, that's if the killer stuck to the plan, there would be more killings in New York before they'd appear in the south. Again, that's only if the criminal acted out his earlier routine. No one had any ideas what his next move would be except for Kal surmising that the murder would happen here, and the instrument would be a needle in the throat. And... if Mr. Invisible followed his latest itinerary, they'd be losing another person most-wanted by the police.

Intending on being involved in these new killings, he contacted the chief of the homicide department in New York and wasn't surprised to find him still working.

"Agent Benson, it's Agent Kal Hunter from the Department of Justice. I understand you're working on a case right now that has come to my attention. I'd like to meet with you as soon as possible."

Chapter Two

June 30th

"What the hell do you mean, you can't go through with it, Sadie? You're in your dream wedding dress. We're in the vestibule of the church, and the bastard, his best man, and the preacher are waiting for you by the altar. Christ, this is like a nightmare rerun of that ridiculous old bride movie when Julia Roberts runs away before the ceremony."

"I know, right? Look, I just can't marry Jon. He's been cheating on me. I caught him back at the hotel last night cuddling with Briana, and they both laughed, said it was just a lark, her wishing him luck or some such bull." Sadie paced swiftly, her long gorgeous gown flashing white silky frills around her like a historical Miss acting out a tirade.

"Why didn't you make a fuss then instead of waiting for the worst possible moment?" Cora's voice rose with every word. "I hate to be a bitch here, but you know it's my weekend to be alone. I've allocated the same time every year, knowing what day is coming soon. You went ahead and planned the wedding for today, and I backed off because I know how much it means to you. But I need to get home and hold my own yearly memorial."

"Your pity party, you mean. It's time you let it go, Cora, more than time. Besides, I need you. You have to help me."

"Okay, okay. If you didn't call him out last night when you found them in a clinch, why now? Just explain that to me, and I'll stop bitching."

"Because he promised me it meant nothing, and I believed him." Sadie swallowed a sob and swiped at her eyes. "Don't you understand? I had faith. I needed to. But I just got a text from Briana." She held out her phone so Cora could see the message.

"She's pregnant? And it's his baby? Are you fucking kidding me?" Cora stared at her best friend, and for once in her life, she had no comeback. That only lasted for as long as it took her to swallow the string of cuss words and then she stuttered, "Yo-you can't marry him."

"I know."

"I don't believe that sick dude intended on going through with the ceremony."

Sadie grabbed Cora's hand and urged her into the side room. She shut the door and swung back to confront Cora who still felt the shock of

Briana's betrayal. Foggy from drinking too much at the family dinner the night before, she let herself be pulled in.

Seeing her pal's white face and the lurking tears, she said the only thing she could say. "What do you want me to do?"

"Give me your dress. I'm going straight to the airport. I have the tickets to Rome and can exchange them for an earlier flight. The suitcases are in my car already, but I can't arrive at the airport looking like this." She held her hands out to show off the white rhinestone-studded filmy gown, with the floor-length skirt cascading masses of ruffles that trailed along the ground.

Turning swiftly, so the backless top with the lace-covered straps and long sleeves were in front of Cora, she growled, "Unzip me. Hurry, Cora."

When Cora didn't move fast enough, Sadie viciously threw her veil across the room and then started ripping her gown off on her own. Yanking frantically at a sleeve, she pulled so hard it tore and hung crookedly.

"What are you doing? Put that back." Cora tried pulling the sleeve up and then slapped Sadie's hands away from the zipper. "Stop it."

"No. I hate this thing now. I just want it off." Sadie turned to Cora. "I need your dress. We're the same size. Hurry. Before someone comes."

Cora, still foggy and feeling completely out of control, continued to argue. "No! Think about what you're doing."

"Think about that bastard sleeping with my so-called partner at the hair salon and getting her pregnant. Then intending on marrying me anyway. Are you crazy?"

Cora suddenly saw the light and changed course. "You're right. Of course, you are. Here let me help you." Stepping to Sadie's back, she pulled down the hidden zipper and helped Sadie get out of the skirts that lay in clouds of white puff all around her feet.

Then she pulled off her jacket to the outfit she'd been so proud of. The one that Sadie hadn't liked for a bridesmaid to wear until Cora showed her the dress alone. Classy, a brilliant royal blue and a gorgeous fit, she agreed it was a style that Cora would get a lot of wear out of, and so she'd given her permission for her to wear a short bridesmaid's dress rather than a long typical gown. Now they were both glad of her choice.

Once Cora had her dress off and helped Sadie with it, handing her the jacket, she stood in her underwear, lacy white panties and bra to match, and reluctantly reached for the dreaded wedding gown, a style she'd never have chosen if it had been a free giveaway and the last one in the store. She slipped it on so Sadie could zip it up. The bulky ruffles played havoc with her normally messy hair.

Sadie grabbed the veil as if to pass it over without any intention of putting it over Cora's spikey hair herself. Realizing what she held, she dropped it as if it were a venomous snake. Next, she grabbed Cora's arms and held them in desperation. "Look, you've got to promise me that you'll go over to the house and get Charli and her pups before you do anything else. That bastard Jon promised we'd take them to a friend's after the ceremony."

"Sure, like that's going to happen now."

"I know. I'm sorry it's too late for me to make different arrangements before I leave, but they can't stay there alone, Cora, and I don't want that asshole anywhere near them. You must promise. My friend, Mona, said she'll take them, but not until tomorrow."

"Yeah, yeah. I'll get them. Here, don't forget your bag with the car keys. Everything's in your suitcases, right? You've got the travel documents and your passport?"

"Yes, everything's there. Even his belongings which I may take time to burn." The thought made them both crack up until Sadie's desperation kicked in again. "I'll leave the car at the airport and take the first plane going in the direction of Miami so I can get there to catch the cruise tomorrow. I bloody paid for most of the trip anyway, I might as well enjoy it rather than waste the money already spent."

"Damn rights, you should. Plus, you'll be safe from all the do-gooders and fussing relatives. I'll deal with them, don't worry. You just have fun and let me know what's happening."

"You'll get Charli. Don't forget."

"I said I would. First thing I'll do when I get out of here. That's after I tell that stinking pile of shit what I think of him, give your mom some smelling salts, and tell your business partner to get her fat, pregnant butt out of your salon. I'm thinking the other girls can keep it going until you return in ten days?"

The sudden banging on the door stopped them from talking. Cora called out, "Hold your horses. We're almost ready. Get everyone seated, and I'll be right out." She hugged Sadie, something she wasn't comfortable doing, but her friend needed the reassurance. "Take off and don't look back."

She watched her weepy friend head to the French doors where she slipped into the gardens and began running for the car.

Wiping away her own commiserating tears, Cora suddenly realized her predicament. A second knock at the door had her scrambling for the huge bouquet of flowers that waited on the side table.

"In a minute. Just wait. We'll be right there."

She quickly grabbed her heels and fixed the mounds of skirt material flying every which way until she eventually got it lying so she could walk without tripping. Snagging the veil and wrapping it around her upper arm, she checked to make sure Sadie had driven away before she stepped into the church vestibule in the direction of the long church room where rows of people were sitting and waiting. As soon as she appeared, the pianist started playing Mendelssohn's Wedding March. And all heads turned her way.

Calling on her police training, she marched up the aisle, a refrain in her head keeping her focused. *Stay calm. You'll feel a lot better afterward.*

Shock came first and then loud voices from the relatives questioning what in the world was happening.

Cora called out, "Remain in your seats, everyone. This will just take a minute." When she finally stood in front of the shocked loser that had pretty-well ruined her best friend's life, she hauled off and slapped him hard with the bouquet she'd brought with her. When he flinched and tried to cover his head, she hit him again harder, and then again.

"That's from Sadie, you sorry son of a bitch. Now, go marry the girl you made pregnant, and be glad I don't have my weapon."

Throwing her floral club at the cowering idiot, she whipped around, skirts flaring, veil flopping behind her, and stomped to the back of the church where she stopped to speak to the flustered congregation. "Hey everyone, there's a lunch spread already paid for next door so you all might as well take advantage."

Having said her piece, she fled across the lawn

to her parked jeep and cussed for having taken the top down on the way to the church. The white frills fought her, but she hastily stuffed as many inside the interior with her as she could and ignored the others that billowed in the wind.

Finally giving up, she ignored the radio playing the loud music she loved and headed over to Sadie's to pick up Charli and her brood of white, fluffy, two-month-old American Eskimo puppies.

Chapter Three

Cora drove a bit crazy, tearing up the road away from the church. She fought with the stupid veil until she got it looped around the steering wheel and it floated out behind her like a flag waving a truce. Her thoughts returned to her white-faced friend who she'd known all her life.

That Sadie couldn't hurt a fly had been known by everyone who ever met the girl. Her heart had been forged with pure gold, and she helped whoever asked for her aid. How could that low-life shithead have pulled the wool over both their eyes for so long?

Thinking back, Cora figured they'd dated for at least four years, and as much as Cora could never cozy up to the jerk, she still would never have believed he had the cheek to have cheated on her friend as he'd done.

One never knew another person and what they

were capable of, that sure as hell came plain as mud today. So much for trusting in a partner who stood at an altar waiting to pledge his love, loyalty, and life to you forever. What a bunch of Hallmark bullshit! Disillusioned, she wished she'd have smacked him harder when she had the chance.

With her mad still raging, she headed for the freeway turnoff. Slowing, as usual, she checked for oncoming traffic. The truck driver heading her way, his eyes bulging, made her grab her wheel and tighten for the crash until at the last second, he seemed to realize where his direction should be and turned off. Not so for the car that came up behind her and slammed into her back bumper.

The sound of a car grinding into hers came seconds before the thrust of her body flung against the steering wheel. Jesus, you'd think no one ever saw a woman in a wedding dress driving a jeep before.

She pulled over, put on the emergency lights, and forced her way out of her car. When her heels caught in the skirt, madder'n a wet hen, she bent down, kicked them off, and threw them into the passenger seat. *Would this torturous day never end? She had an appointment with a bottle of rum and no time for such nonsense.*

With that nasty attitude in place, she stomped barefoot to the car behind her, the young female driver waiting for her on the sidewalk. Shocked, shaking, her face a picture of remorse, and her eyes fighting the tears, the overweight twenty-something-year-old spoke first. "It's all my fault. I'm so sorry. I was in an accident earlier this week, and I'm still shaky. I wa-wasn't careful." Staring at the wedding gown as if Cora were an alien from another planet, she clutched her hands and started to cry. "Please... I'm so sorry."

Cora glanced at the back of her Jeep and saw a small smudge on the bumper, hardly visible, but she pointed at it as if it were a huge dent. "Look what you did to my car. You could have killed me." Knowing she needed to make her point, she ignored the pity that welled up and instead glanced through the open window to the front passenger seat where a cellphone lay open. "Were you playing around with that sucker?"

"No! No ma'am, I swear, I'd never do that."

"Yeah, sure. So, if I checked your photos, I wouldn't see a picture of my car you were probably taking instead of paying attention to your driving?"

Guilt flooded, mixing with the tears and Cora had her answer.

"Seriously, kid? What were you thinking? Where's your head? Second accident this week, and you didn't learn your lesson after the first time?"

Hands covering her face, a picture of remorse, the forlorn girl whispered, "I wasn't driving the first time. I swear. I'm sorry. I never saw a bride driving an open jeep before."

Knowing she must have been a sight since even the trucker had reacted, she still wouldn't let up. Taking her phone from the pocket in the dress that Sadie had insisted on the bridal shop adding – Sadie never went anywhere without her cell – Cora made her voice hard. "Where's your driver's license and registration? If there's any cost to fixing my ride, you'll be paying the shot, not me."

The girl couldn't give her the documents fast enough, her squeaky voice promising, "Whatever it costs, I'll pay for it. I'll be more than happy to take care of your repairs. Here's my phone number," she dictated the number and her email address while Cora took her time on purpose, wanting to give the driver as much leeway to settle down as she could before she let her drive away.

Her last shot at the trembler had her face whitening even more. "I'm Detective Cora Taylor with the NOPD. I have your information, and I'll be setting a red mark beside your name with the license bureau. If there are any other incidents with your driver's info in the next five years, you'll be riding a bike. Got it?" Knowing it for the bogus nonsense it really was didn't matter, it was the threat that worked the magic.

"Yes, ma'am. I'm so sorry." Pointing at the ripped, hanging sleeve of the wedding dress, she added, "And I'm sorry about your wedding... ahh, problems too."

"Yeah, well, shit happens, kiddo. Now drive responsibly."

Heading back to her car, Cora felt the hot pavement burn into her bare feet. There was no anger to cover it up this time. Wincing and prancing till she got back behind the wheel, she didn't see how comical a barefoot bride in full regalia could look.

Not until the YouTube video came out and the guys in the precinct were happy to show it to her some days later. Bloody phones were everywhere nowadays.

Chapter Four

"So, who are you taking with you on this wild criminal search in New Orleans for the cold-case killer, Streak?"

"Jesus, Shawn, I wished you were still here working with me. I'd know my back was covered, no second-guessing. This dude they slapped me with last month has about as much humor as... as Sam."

"Hey, quit disparaging my canine friend. He laughs. I've seen him roll his eyes over your stupid ass many times."

"Very cute."

"And between us, I still don't know what he sees in you that he's hung around all this time. I'd steal the pooch if I thought he'd come with me down south."

"Are we talking about the same mutt? The annoying furball that follows me home every night? Sure, he shows enthusiasm and even giddiness, but that's only when he spots food. He has no sense of the ridiculous."

"I beg to differ. He chose you to be his owner, an OCD fanatic who vacuums around his body every few seconds in case any fur gets loose in your pristine loft. The dog's gotta have some comedy inside that big ole body."

"Ha! Not funny, man. I'm serious. Look, I'm telling you this newest killing spree is driving me nuts. People are dying, and so far, we haven't been able to do a thing to stop it. I figure I've lost ten pounds from working overtime and lack of sleep. Not that I'm complaining."

"Okay, keep cool, son. I know you and your crazy work ethic. You say to date, the killer has taken out lowlifes and bad guys, right? Maybe he's a vigilante freak? Nothing to do with the first guy who murdered innocent people... and for who knows why. Since we never caught up with the sick prick, his reasons never came to light."

"Bullshit. This son of a bitch wouldn't know the order of the earlier kills or each method used because we kept some of those factors to ourselves. Remember? We did so on purpose so there wouldn't be any copycat follow-ups."

"Right. And we never caught him. Could be, he's returned to his old tricks, but this time he wants to make the deaths count."

"Seriously? It's just like you to give our freak

motivations for carrying out his unspeakable acts. He's a killing machine and needs to be caught. End of argument."

"And I've no doubt that you and what's his name, funny-man Freddie, will take him down. I'm hoping it's not before he rids the globe of more of the lowlifes he's offed. Oops! Gotta go, my friend. The surf is calling."

"Yeah, go hit the waves you lazy beach bum. Don't give a thought to your best pal busting his butt, trying to catch a murdering lowlife. Have a beer on me."

"Not gonna work, Kallie. I don't feel bad for you whatsoever. Just glad I seen the light in time so I could enjoy what's still to come."

"Yeah, thanks to your grandma's will leaving you her estate, lucky prick."

"That too. Take care of Sammie. Give him an extra chewy bone for me."

"Right. See you soon as I get this case solved. I'll be needing vacation time by then."

"Hope it's this year, dude." Kal heard the laughter and then the voice adding, "Just fuckin' wit'cha, son. Stay safe."

Sad to end the call with his old partner, Kal got serious and began making decisions. He'd be traveling soon, his destination New Orleans. If the old schedule followed suit, the next kill would happen there. He began cleaning up his desk and making a lot of notes he'd be leaving with his secretary for the others in the department.

The non-stop barrage of killings they'd been unable to curtail had given him a lot of sleepless nights. He'd been right in suspecting the killer would follow his previous methods. So far, he'd used a needle in the throat of a known pedophile who'd been at his dirty little tricks again but hadn't divulged enough evidence for them to make an arrest.

Then he'd bludgeoned his next prey, a well-known pervert who was highly suspected of trafficking young women. They'd been four steps behind on that case, and every officer working that specific task force would have given a week's wage to have been the one to have stopped him. Though no one specifically cheered, plenty were walking lighter knowing the sicko was off the streets for good.

A few weeks later, he'd chosen to rid the world of a whacky arsonist who'd begun setting his sneaky little fires a month or so after being released early from a twenty-year sentence. Three houses had been destroyed with numerous wounded and one man dead. Picking up the suspected culprit, their plans to prosecute had been thwarted when he produced alibis for the time of all three fires. Considering they'd all started the same way, by small explosions detonated from a distance, his defense might not have stood up in a court of law.

When each explosion happened, the area all

around each home had enough fire-catching gas and exploding materials for it to expand and consume the buildings quickly. Unfortunately, whether they sensed he'd performed the unspeakable acts or not, the evidence hadn't been enough to make an arrest.

Though they weren't able to hold him after questioning, he'd later been found with a plastic bag around his head, while his hands were tied behind him – same as victim number five in the original deaths. What they all noted to date... no more fires.

On and on it went. Killing after killing. They could never get ahead of the cold-case monster. As much as they had difficulty regretting his choice of victims, they knew it was their responsibility to put a stop to his rampage.

But they had no idea who carried out the assassinations or who the next target would be. Every murder scene was tampered with, so evidence became minimal. The criminal never made a mistake or left them any clues at all. It was like he knew what they'd be looking for and made sure they'd never find a thing that could lead them to him.

It drove Kal crazy.

As the guy now in charge, he decided who came with him to New Orleans. And it seemed only smart to bring along his young partner, Fred, yet begrudged the need. If the guy hadn't such computer skills that made his own look dismal, he'd have thought twice. But they might be needed, and he'd be kicking his own butt if he got there and missed not having the tech genius nearby.

These were the times he missed Shawn the most. If they still worked together, he'd have been thrilled to plan the travel arrangements. Unfortunately, this new guy seemed to have the same limited humor as Sam no matter what Shawn had to say about the dog's intelligence.

He stopped his brooding to look at his pet and felt instant loyalty. As if he sensed Kal's discontent, Sam stretched to his feet, laid his head against Kal's thigh as if to say, what do you need?

Reaching to pet the suddenly energetic animal, he appreciated the hand wash and secretly agreed with Shawn that even Sam got more fun out of the ridiculous than the stick-in-the-mud they'd forced on him last month. Giving the devil his due, he hoped that some people just needed time before they'd relax and act human.

Shrugging, Kal stopped bemoaning Shawn's early retirement. Though he'd worked with Shawn for the last seven years since he'd taken the position as an agent for the FBI, he had to let go of the past. As hard as it was for him, the now happy man had retired before his time to follow his dream, live in Sayulita, a hip little village on the coast in Mexico, and be a sun bunny rum drinker for the rest of his days.

Accepting these new facts had been difficult for a guy who hated change. But Shawn had given him no choice. He'd pulled the plug before he'd shared the news. Facing the done deal, forced to accept the inevitable, Kal had caved and wished his buddy good luck.

Now, Shawn, who knew him inside out and laughed at his worst jokes, was only a call away. It would be a home to go to for the holidays like they'd discussed.

Shaking off his uglies, Shawn's name for Kal's moodiness, he grinned at the latest postcard propped up against his desk lamp with the half-naked, wrinkly seventy-year-old bathing beauty on the front and shook his head. The guy always could make him laugh.

Kal hated change, he'd admit it. And progress be damned. Why couldn't life stay the same instead of knocking a guy sideways just when everything ran smooth?

His glance landed on the open files in front of him and once again he noticed the picture of the twenty-three-year-old patrol officer, her fresh young face being the perfect backdrop for her scared, sad, blue eyes.

Chapter Five

Cora couldn't get up off the kitchen floor. Whether it was the stupid gown she'd left on from the night before or the stupid pups who crawled all over the stupid frills, playfully biting at them as if they were the best pull toys ever, she wasn't certain.

Most likely it was the half-empty bottle of rum she still held in her hand that had turned her legs to rubber. Afraid to open her eyes, she went to lift her empty left hand to rub at the dried tears on her cheeks, but her lack of energy forbid the movement. Or maybe it was one of the pups who'd curled inside her palm for warmth that created such heaviness that moving seemed impossible.

Her pickled brain didn't shut down as it had the last three times she'd woken slightly. Of course, a few more gulps of the devil rum probably had something to do with her passing out yet again so her brain could maintain the necessary haze she needed to get through these two days.

Every year, she dreaded the first long weekend of July, and this year more so since her supposedly best friend had planned her wedding to take place on the very weekend Cora always indulged in memories of her worst nightmare. Her indulgence taking the shape of a weekend long binge with her old friend rum.

Her boss knew to book her off for these days. Her once a year trip to the liquor store meant the most expensive rum bottle would be in her cupboard to help her live through the horrendous worst days of her life where four people died because she hadn't done her job.

No excuse, no sympathy, not like what others said to her so she wouldn't lose her mind. Especially her then and still now boss, Deputy Larry Swanson. He'd been a Lieutenant back in those days, one who had the hots for her when she was a rookie. Over the years, she'd finally persuaded him that though she appreciated his support, especially during the bleakest days in her life, she wasn't bride material.

After the sham of this weekend, it became more firmly embedded in her brain that the weakest gender wasn't to be trusted. As a modern woman of today, she'd stick to being single, running her own life, and never being at the beck and call of any self-satisfying prick who thought he could call the shots.

Bleary-eyed, she turned her head very carefully

to see if the puppies still had water and food. Considering she'd left scads of pee-pads all over the kitchen and bowls filled with water and food under the table, she decided she'd done her due diligence for Sadie's dogs.

Hell, she'd even come to sit with them giving up her comfy sofa when they'd started howling for attention. Now that's attentiveness over and above doggy sitting rules. Sadie owed her big-time.

As if she sensed her human awake, Charli, the puppies' mother, trotted over to lick Cora on the face, as if commiserating with her once again. Dreams of the same treatment occurring periodically during the last twenty-four hours came back to Cora. She kind of remembered having more than one good cry while cuddling one of the baby furballs in her arms and receiving unreserved loving in return. Having her face washed and a furry head tucked into her neck had felt good at the time. Drunk as she'd been, she'd wallowed in the attention and affection.

Now that her brain had started re-functioning with some semblance of lucidity, she decided she'd just close her eyes for a few more seconds in memory of the family who'd lost their lives because she hadn't pulled the trigger. One last grievance before she resumed her life to carry on until next year. One last torrent of tears.

As if her eyes received their orders, they poured out their pain, and her heart seized yet again. So much sadness flooded her being that even if she'd wanted to, she couldn't have moved. The pup sensed yet again the swell of unmitigated grief. She moved in close to snuggle and do her job of cuddling while giving sympathy to the person who'd become important in her world.

She licked and nuzzled while Cora sprawled on the floor. Once the woman had cried herself dry, she'd passed out again. Yet Charli's baby had stayed in her arms until she heard the truck pull into the driveway.

Chapter Six

Agent Kal looked over at Deputy Larry Swanson, the same man who used to be a lieutenant ten years ago. The man who'd fought so hard for Officer Cora Taylor, while others couldn't suppress the blame they felt against her incompetence.

Thinking about the episode, he reminisced how Cora had caught up with the perp as he'd been fleeing from his latest murder of a store clerk. A machete had been the weapon of choice used for that kill. And he'd left that at the scene as per his regular tactic. Yet, for the first time, they'd later found out that he'd seized a rifle from the hands of the clerk and absconded with it.

Officer Cora Taylor had somehow found his trail behind the garage convenience store and had followed him through the woods, calling in her whereabouts so they were close on her heels. According to what had come out later, she'd caught up to him, and they'd fought. She'd tripped him and tried to pin him to the ground, but he'd flipped her off. Then he'd kicked her in the face, stomped on her stomach, and would have probably killed her if she hadn't had the foresight to grab for her gun.

"Stop right there. Back off." She'd stumbled to her feet to fall over again, giving him the chance to back away.

He'd picked up the rifle he'd dropped and took off while she'd begged him to stop. "Don't make me shoot." The sicko had hesitated and laughed maniacally, his words ringing out so those approaching had heard them too. "Shoot me. Do it, girl. I won't stop if you don't. You have the power, you're the only one. So... shoot that fucking gun."

He'd screamed those last words, his voice raw with pain, and to this day, on nights when overtiredness brought terrible dreams, Kal heard them repeated in his sleep. The sound of a man suffering extreme agony, begging for release. And she hadn't pulled the trigger. She'd froze, and the killer had disappeared into the woods before he'd been able to take the shot himself.

Though they'd followed, each of their team spreading out, Kal with Officer Taylor and detective Swanson, they hadn't been in time. They'd stumbled on to his trail and an hour later had heard shots in the distance. By the time they'd arrived at the house, four bodies waited.

And a nightmare began.

It had been the only time the felon hadn't varied

his killings by using a different weapon. Unless one counted the fact that he'd used the rifle he'd stolen, rather than the handgun like in the first crime. Still, no prints. Nothing to work with. Same as the other crime scenes.

Other than the bodies that had been fired on from the living room doorway while the family of four had lounged on the couch watching TV, there'd been nothing to give the officers any clues whatsoever. No tire marks, no footprints, nothing. It was like the killer had suddenly appeared, did the dirty, and then floated off on a cloud.

After they'd penetrated the family home where the four killings had taken place, something in Kal had made him stop. Coming up behind him was Cora Taylor, refusing to let her injuries stop her from doing her job.

He'd caught the injured, white-faced, shaking woman close before she'd entered the room. He'd held her head against his chest so she couldn't see the bodies – tried to force her from the place so the images wouldn't sear into her brain the way they had in his.

But she'd fought him, even with her face all bruised. Pushed against his arms and struggled so much, he'd been forced to let go. Her wail of grief would never leave him. She'd known those bodies were there because she hadn't given a begging-for-death crazy man his wish.

She hadn't pulled the trigger.

***

In later days, they'd tried their hardest to catch the murdering bastard, pulling out all the stops, searching every household in the small county, checking every motel and hotel possible.

Hunting for the killer, they watched the train station, planes, buses, and had roadblocks on all the major highways and backroads entering the area. Knowing the healthy shipping industry could also be a place to disappear, they spent even more time combing through each terminal, taking no chances, exploring each possible angle of escape.

Every officer in the area worked overtime willingly to find and catch the killing machine... only they never did. The culprit, who according to Officer Taylor, wore a grey sweatshirt with the hood over his head so she couldn't tell his hair coloring or his facial proportions.

Other than she knew he was a white man of medium build, the color of his eyes, or any markings they could have used were never seen because of the dark and the distance. Even his voice had been distorted by screams. In the end, all they had to go on was the fact that the murdering bastard had been a male. And in the same way they'd found with every one of his previous kills, neither the machete nor the rifle gave any clues to the man who'd used them.

Over the next week, Officer Taylor had been in the hospital suffering from the beating she'd taken, and her treatment had kept her from the office. Kal had approached then Captain Joe Mason with the explicit request that Officer Taylor be given her dismissal, mainly based on the fact that she wasn't suited for her position as a cop.

By refusing to pull the trigger, she'd endangered the rest of the officers that day as well as the people who'd been killed. He argued the responsibility had been too much for the sensitive young woman.

It wasn't because he wanted revenge for her hesitation. Nothing like that. If the truth were known, the idea of that big-eyed angel having to face murderers and thugs every day seemed obscene to him. He'd rather picture her working a safe job with nice people. Though he'd never talked to her again, he'd visited her in the hospital only to find her asleep.

In that light, her injuries showed clearly, her poor face a mass of bruises and cuts. He'd had the silliest urge to lie beside her, cuddle her close and never let her be hurt again.

But she lived in a different world from his, one he'd be leaving soon. He only hoped the words he'd left with her bosses would be enough for them to persuade her she needed a new profession. Of course, there'd been arguments from Lieutenant Swanson on behalf of his rookie, but Kal figured out quickly the guy had the hots for the female cop and the decision wouldn't be his alone.

Even Captain Mason had been very

complimentary over her abilities, the top marks from her trainers, the academy, and all her teachers, so that he'd made no promises, but would look at all the facts, talk to everyone involved and base his decision for her future on those.

Though Kal's recommendation would of course be taken into consideration, he had to understand that he had no jurisdiction over their station and the final choice would have to be made once they'd talked to the officer herself.

Fine. He'd left it alone then, knowing he'd done whatever he could to protect the poor girl from ever having to go through a similar nightmare in the future. As time moved on, he'd returned to his position in New York and had eventually been recruited by the FBI.

Ten years had passed before he'd returned.

Once back in New Orleans, he'd found a lot of changes. The Captain had moved into the Deputy Superintendent's slot while Detective Joe Mason now held the Captain's position for the Eighth District. And... one of his best employees, who they were driving to see at the moment, was no other than *Lieutenant* Cora Taylor.

According to the man sporting a wedding ring and a proud smile, not only had she remained in the police force, but she'd excelled and was one of their most highly thought of officers.

Chapter Seven

Kal had never before been greeted at an unlocked door by a fluffball of white exuberance. Upon entering Cora Taylor's home, hit with the doggy smell he knew well enough from his own place, they stepped into the kitchen and could see why the odor had lingered.

A woman, her short blonde hair sticking out all over her head, tears messing with closed eyes completely covered in mascara and eyeliner running over her tear-dried cheeks, lay propped against the wall. A ruffled white wedding gown spilled around her body as she was spread-eagled on the floor, one ripped satin sleeve hanging loose.

An empty bottle of expensive rum was clutched in the right hand while one of the multiple pups snoozed in the left. Other fluffies were curled into her skirts, the ruffles hiding their bodies until they moved, stumbling forward on fat little legs to get their portion of attention. He counted five in all until the mother dog moved into her position of protection. Her lips growled a warning toward him as if she was worried he was planning to mess with her mistress.

Stunned, he stood back, having to use the counter for support. My Lord, he wanted so badly to pull out his phone and take a shot of the indescribable scene. The man with him began to chuckle under his breath before he turned to Kal. "It's Cora's weekend. I forgot."

"Does she do this every weekend?" Stunned, he asked the question, hoping the answer would clear up his vision of a cop suffering a really bad problem.

"God, no. It's only one weekend each year – you know, close to the same one as ten years ago when the first killing happened. She handles this time in her own way – gets drunk and lives through the three days as best she can. Only this year her best friend Sadie got married, so she has the wedding dress on."

"Wait, if her friend Sadie was getting married, why does Cora have on the dress?"

"Because Sadie found out that her fiancé, Jon, got Briana, her partner at their hair salon, pregnant and ran away before the ceremony. Guess they changed clothes before she headed to the airport, leaving Cora to deal with the groom and the guests. Gotta say it was a humdinger watching

Cora beat the bastard with the bouquet before she told the rest of us to enjoy the luncheon and then hightailed it outta there to come home and hide away for the rest of the time."

Captain Swanson, Larry, finally leaned down to pick up one of the squalling pups. He petted the fussing mother dog so she wouldn't fret. "It's okay, Charli. I won't hurt your babies."

She'd backed down when it was Larry who'd moved in and not the stranger she seemed wary of. "This one is going to be our baby once she's weaned."

Just as Kal felt his head would explode, Cora opened her bleary eyes and stared at the two men. Words spoken in a rusty tone of indignant reprisal were not quite whispered, but close. "Get out of my house, or I'll get my gun."

"Now she's going to shoot." Kal's muttered words made Larry grin, but he ignored him and bent down to the woman. "Honey, no one's shooting anyone. We need your help, so get your shit together and clean yourself up."

Cora moved her hand, and realizing she still held a puppy, she gently lowered it to rest on her skirt. Dropping the empty rum bottle, she raised her hands to her eyes, her clenched fists leaving more of a mess on her colorful cheeks.

Dried tears destroyed the kaleidoscope of blues and purples that had once graced her eyes. The streaks of black that had been mascara and eyeliner in another life made her look like a desperate rock star who'd gone wild with her makeup.

Seeing that the men weren't going to budge, she tried to stand, only to fall over from the weight of the heavy crinoline skirt and the pups still using it as their mattress.

Larry reached down to scatter a couple of the pups, while Kal lifted the one nearest him only to get his face washed from the fluffy white handful. Sad for having to put it down, he lowered it close to where the food bowls had been filled but were now destroyed with pellets scattered everywhere.

Pointing toward the man who earned a scowl, Cora spoke in a strained voice. "Who's the stranger you brought into my house?" Struggling to get to her feet, she fell back in a mound of tangled satin skirts, her bare legs showing among the mess of satin and crinoline. Before he could answer, she waved her hand. "Never mind. Just help me up, and then find me some Tylenol. I mean a bottle of the sons of bitches. I need a shower. And grab those fucking puppies before they get into the rest of the place and shit everywhere. Call Mona and tell her to get her ass over here. She was supposed to pick up the little bastards the day after the wedding."

"It is the day after the wedding. She probably tried to get your attention, but you'd be too drunk to answer your phone, Rookie."

"Bull. She knows where I keep the keys. You

did."

"The door was open when I got here."

"See!"

Scratching his head, seeming to know better than to argue, Larry asked, his tone reasonable, "Did you hear anyone knocking?"

As if his words got through, she slammed her hand on the wall to stop from falling over and whirled around to face him. "Shit. Do I have to do everything around here? Whatever. Call her."

"Say please, and I might."

"How about I say go fuck yourself?"

Laughing as if he'd heard the biggest joke ever, Larry nodded. "Go get cleaned up, honeybunch. I brought an old friend of yours, but he wouldn't recognize you today. Hell, I'm having trouble myself. Never thought I'd see you wearing a wedding dress, Rookie."

Cora stopped struggling to walk, pulling at the skirts, and cussing under her breath. She turned and glared at Kal, then lowered her head as if she had no idea or gave a damn who he was.

If Kal hadn't have been so close, he wouldn't have seen her eyes widen or her cracked lips clutch her teeth as if to hold in a cry. Then she'd swung around so quickly, her skirts almost pulled her down before she struggled to get the crinoline and ruffles through the doorway into the other part of the house.

He managed to grab the same puppy who'd

nestled in her hand and who suddenly began to follow the woman who'd given her warmth and been so gentle. The baby cried in frustration, struggling to shadow the one she'd chosen as hers.

Kal knew exactly how the wriggler felt...

Chapter Eight

Cora hadn't believed her own eyes, thought it had been a figment of her drunken hangover or some weird imagination trick. After all, she'd spent the last twenty-four hours or so reliving ten years ago, and that man had played one of the major roles in her memories.

The very man who'd metaphorically stabbed her in the back now stood in her kitchen, the sorry prick. Ten years earlier, he'd been the one who demanded they fire her ass. He'd even passed over her immediate supervisor to talk to Joe Mason, the Captain of the Eighth District then.

It had been a close call. If she hadn't actually fought with the maniac killer, trying to bring him down physically, she still believed they would have reached a different conclusion.

Also, Detective Larry Swanson had saved her ass by sticking up for her as a rookie. No one could expect perfection from someone who'd been on the team for less than a year, had never had reason to pull her gun, and had up till then shown such promise.

To repay their faith in her abilities, she'd become their best detective, worked harder and longer hours than any in the district, and to this day, had spent ridiculous amounts of time trying to unmask the cold-case-killer. If anyone saw the room in her basement that held every piece of information she'd retrieved over the years about that case, every photo, and police file, they might think her a weird conspiracy theorist over the dude.

Maybe if they'd caught the scum bastard, she could let it go. But that had never happened. Since the killings had been prevalent in New York, and more people had periodically worked the case for months, maybe years, she knew they had little to show from their efforts.

In her research, she'd seen that Detective Kal Hunter had been active until he'd moved to join the FBI. Then both he and his partner, Agent Shawn Bonaire, had still dug in from time to time, especially lately. Yet little had been found and the case had remained cold. Until the killings resumed...

Dragging the torn gown off her body, pulling at the layers of satin and ruffles, crinolines, and slips that clung, she almost lost her cookies. Running into the bathroom, she gave herself permission to let the sickness out once and for all, rather than fight to keep it inside. Other than the pounding in her head and the rotten taste in her mouth, her tummy sent its thanks for having rid itself of the noxious, disgusting mess.

Funny how those first few mouthfuls of rum always tasted so good until the numbness struck and nothing mattered anymore. No cares about her physical self or the promise of the worst hangover in the world. Only what transpired in her sad, sorry mind. It wasn't as if she could ever let herself be seen in such a condition. Heavens, she'd never let others she respected know how low she'd go one weekend every year.

Appreciating that Larry wouldn't have interrupted her time off for any small reason and bringing that blasted ghost along with him made her take notice.

She couldn't believe that the same agent who'd caused her heart to swell and foolish dreams to emerge ten years ago looked as well as he did today.

Manly, slim but wiry, his muscled body had shown the strength of a person who took good care of himself. She'd known the heat had gotten to him when he'd left his suit jacket off, had pulled his tie loose, and his wrinkled white shirt stuck in places to his honed body. New Orleans heat could do that to an unsuspecting victim.

In comparison to her drunken appearance at the worst moment possible, she had nothing to brag about herself. All she knew was that God had a mean sense of humor.

Pulling her thoughts from the man who'd shared many of her dreams over the years, she concentrated on why he'd arrived in her territory again.

Whoever had continued the sudden copy-cat killings in New York hadn't wavered from the uniformity of the first onslaught. He'd continued his slayings exactly as they'd occurred ten years earlier, same weapons, same days of the week – of course with different victims. It wasn't surprising he'd be following his nemesis's trail to New Orleans.

Unlike others, she didn't believe the real murderer had begun his shenanigans again. It had been ten long years, why would he suddenly become active and start that nightmare over?

Others might believe, but she'd heard the weariness in his voice, still heard it in nightmares periodically. The self-loathing and the need he'd had for release. He'd wanted to die; wanted her to kill him, of that she had no doubt. When the carnage had stopped abruptly, it made a sick kind of sense... though, to this day, she wished she'd pulled that fucking trigger.

Straightening, she glanced in the mirror. Grabbing the edge of the sink, the vision that stared back at her almost did her in. Lord love a duck; she'd never looked worse. Makeup splattered everywhere in streaks all over her face, her hair a perfect version of a blonde rat's nest.

Heading for the shower, she dropped the rest of the clothes from her weary body and let the last of the tears mix with the hot water where no one would see her rare weakness. Hardened beyond what she ever thought herself capable of, swearing her anger rather than her earlier rookie ways of polite conversation, she worked through each day, becoming the cynical police officer who needed to do the daily job of handling rough, tough criminals who cared less for law enforcement as the years went on.

Not that she didn't draw the line for over-zealous handling of perps, she believed in boundaries, but she often bemoaned the fact that many of the folks on the wrong side of the law had little or no respect for law enforcement and it showed in their disillusioned behavior.

There remained one saving grace and work that mattered, which gave her peace of mind. She spent many of her non-working hours in the assisted living facility in her neighborhood. It had started when her mother had moved there after losing her second husband.

Never understanding how those two had bonded, Cora's asshole stepdad had ruled her mother's world for years. Truth be told, he'd been her mother's choice of a second-chance hubby, and they seemed to have had a decent life together.

He'd never have been hers. In her mind, he couldn't hold a candle to her own Detective father who they'd lost years before.

This guy's loud, bullshitting ways had turned her off early in their relationship, but respect for her mother had continued to bring her around. Usually, she'd plan her visits when he'd be at work, and then later in his retirement, she'd get his golf-playing schedule and fit her drop-overs in during his constant evening playdates when it would be cool enough to hit the fairway.

Because her mother had been so good to her, had taught her right from wrong and how to respect and appreciate her pluses rather than take them for granted, she loved spending time with her. Affectionate and kind, always looking on the bright side, Dawn had been everything a girl needed in a parent.

When she'd lost her second husband and found herself alone in her later years, Cora had finally gotten up the gumption to question her second choice. "Mom, what made you marry a man so opposite to Dad?"

"I loved your father, Cora, desperately. Yet every day he went to work was a day in hell for me. I worried myself sick thinking of all the ways he could be harmed on the job. Turns out, I was right to worry. He was shot while at work. That's when I made up my mind that I would never again take the chance of being with any man who's career would demand him being at risk. When I met Bob, he seemed kind, harmless, and his every wish was to make me happy. I never had to be afraid to breathe when he left the house." Cora heard the unspoken end of the sentence – *not like you* – and changed the subject.

When they discovered that Bob hadn't been as frugal with money as he'd led them to believe, Cora gladly helped pay the expenses for her mom to live out the rest of her time in assisted comfort, surrounded by her peers.

A decision to drop over there sometime either today or tomorrow seemed important. Her mother had always been aware of what went down on these yearly weekends, and she'd worry herself into a mess until Cora let her know it was over and she hadn't done anything stupid.

Not only did her mom fret, but now she had half the joint worrying with her. Until Cora showed up in one piece and proved to them she was fine, they wouldn't settle, and she'd be in trouble with the staff for days.

All the while she speculated, she gathered her work clothes, including black linen slacks and the white T-shirts she wore with them, her holster that sat on her hip, and the lanyard with her badge.

As usual, her hair gave her trouble, sticking out everywhere, and as her typical way of dealing with it, she grabbed the scissors close by and snipped off the fronds that wouldn't stay in place.

Now it really stuck out. Jesus, why couldn't she enjoy getting a hairdresser to deal with the shit? Plastered to a chair while other hands worked with her hair maddened her to where she had to hold her tongue. So, she lived with the messy look, never realizing how quaint and cute others found it and how many tried to copy the look.

Her makeup took a while longer as she had a lot to cover. The strain lines around her eyes seemed deeper, looking more drawn. The slathering on of the eye shadow, mascara, and eyeliner, gave one a vision of a person hiding rather than revealing the image of someone modern or sleek.

More like a woman scared and tearful who wouldn't let anyone close because she didn't deserve to be loved. Not after what she'd done... or failed to do. How could she live a normal life when her inaction had been responsible for the death of a beautiful family?

Hell, she had a hard time living with herself. Sure as shit, no one else would want to be with her day after day, dealing with her guilt and pain.

Chapter
Nine

Kal waited with Larry, following his example. While Larry had Mona on the line, telling her to come now to collect the canine brood, he rolled up the various well-used puppy pads and put them in a plastic bag he'd found near the garbage can. The kitchen had a well-used look about it, obviously clean, but still with a controlled mess that a lot of folks like to live in.

It was nothing like his kitchen where everything had labels, a place of its own and had to be put there, or he couldn't settle. Life wasn't fun with that particular monkey riding his back. Being a person with such limitations had always had its downfalls. Not many women could put up with the fussiness. It drove them crazy, so they'd pick up and leave. Others, who had no trouble with his finicky ways, soon grew tiresome with their bemoaning his hours. Those were the ones he'd ask to leave.

Now, with big ugly Sam in the picture, none of his women friends wanted to share his space. None he'd met so far.

Once free from his phone call, Larry began rounding up the scattering pups. Between the two of them, they hauled them out into the yard, having to watch them closely as there was no fence to pen them in.

At first, the mother, Charli, had fretted at the door to Cora's room along with one of her pups, but soon came with them once she understood her babies would be going outside. Free on the grass, they scampered in all directions with the big officers scrambling after them.

"Come here you little devil." Kal restrained another fleeing canine heading under their SUV while still having one in his hand. He spotted an empty box by the door and quickly procured it as their temporary home. Once all five pups were secure and Charli nestled in the box with them, Kal took the moment to scan the area.

Cora had a large yard, lots of fig and orange trees, and a whole wall to the side where bougainvillea rioted with various colors fighting for prominence. He saw a face peeking through the hedge at the back and made out a nosy neighbor with no self-control and who cared less if she got caught snooping.

Kal's motioning his head got Larry's attention who yelled out teasingly, "Hey Nora, you want to come all the way over and see what's happening here? It must be hard standing on tippy toes to snoop."

"You calling me nosy, Deputy Swanson?" The indignant tone of her voice reeked with insult. "Why I'm just clipping my hedge."

Cora's sudden interruption left nothing for the listener to surmise. "Right... with no clippers. You're being freakin' nosy, Nora, and we all know it, so back off and mind your own business." She nailed it right off the bat.

"And you need to wash out your mouth, you bad girl. I'll be telling your mother about this, see if I don't."

"Right. Fine. Sorry for the poopy mouth. Just don't worry Mom right now."

The silence suddenly filled with a loud sigh. "I forgot, it's THE weekend. I'm sorry too, sweet girl. You be careful now. Ya hear?"

"I hear. Thanks, Nora." Cora motioned the men to follow her back into the house, whispering, "She won't go away. It's best to talk inside." Charli instantly returned to her side, jumping up for attention. Without her beside them, the pups began wailing their disagreement for being left alone. "Bring the brats or we won't be able to hear ourselves think."

Kal had tried to hide his shock of her appearance, but Larry caught the stunned expression on his face and whispered, "Meet the real Detective Cora Taylor, my man. She's a hot commodity around here, so don't mess with her or you'll answer to me and my crew."

Once they all returned to the kitchen, the pups still crowded in the box with Charli leaning over the side to calm them, Cora headed straight for her fancy coffee machine on the counter and plugged in the espresso option. Reaching into her cupboard, she withdrew three mugs, all with humorous sayings on the front.

Kal noticed that no matter what the momma dog did to settle her litter, one of the little nuisances wouldn't settle down. She kept jumping at the edge, trying desperately to get out of her confinement. Every time she heard Cora speak, asking what the others wanted to drink, she howled her dissatisfaction.

Suddenly, Charli ran to Cora, and standing on her hind legs, she begged with her eyes and even her whines.

Feeling ridiculous, yet understanding the frantic dog's signals, Kal translated, "She's asking you to help her baby. It's you the pup's crying for."

Kal couldn't believe that it was so obvious to him and yet Cora seemed unaware of what the hell was happening. She'd kindly patted Charli, even shushed her, gently urging her to go be with her offspring, but it hadn't hit home that she was wanted so desperately that the heartbroken puppy wasn't going to stop.

Finally, reaching the end of his patience, he rescued the little one and as soon as he picked her up, she wriggled free. Rolling, running, she staggered her way to the woman standing with shock written all over her face. Determined for Cora to pay attention, she tried to climb up her leg. The tearful beseeching stare wasn't hard to decipher. She wanted to be cuddled by only one person. And that person wouldn't soften.

"Larry put the puppy back with the others."

"Nope. She wants you."

"I don't want a puppy. I have no time for a dog, you know that. I can't encourage her, you numbskull. Fucking put her back in the box."

"Nope. You do it."

Cora glared at Kal. "Hey city boy, do something for your coffee. Put this little devil back with the others."

Kal looked into the narrow-eyed stare from blue gazers that could make a man weep and shook his head. Then he crossed his arms to stop from weakening. "Sorry."

"Shit." By now the pup had worked herself into a terrible mess and the screeching wails were deafening. She meant to be listened to. She knew what she wanted, and no one would be dissuading her.

Cora bent over and pointed her finger close to the little black nose. "You, be quiet! Stop that nonsense."

The crying came to an abrupt end. The baby sat back on its haunches, fell over, quickly sat again, and this time managed to stay in place. It stared up at the woman with a face full of adoration, waiting.

"Oh, give me a break." Cora leaned down and stared right into the eyes of her avid fan. "You can't stay with me. I'm never home. You be a good girl and go with the others."

The pup turned her head as if she wouldn't listen anymore. Then she began her crying again, the screeching grew louder every second Cora refused to be nice. Charli, worried about her heartbroken baby, tried to quiet it, licking its face, and with her nose, urged her away from Cora, but the stubborn little furball ran around her mother and back at Cora.

"Son of a bitch, and I mean that literally. You're just determined to mess up my life." Cora picked up the baby and everyone watched as it settled into her hands as if home had arrived. Then it licked at Cora, rubbing its face against her arm.

Just then a knock could be heard before an older woman bustled in without waiting for her hostess to come to the door. "So, where's the litter I promised to look after?"

Chapter Ten

Cora couldn't believe that she still felt guilty about forcing Mona to take all the pups with her. The one who'd decided she was Cora's had fought, cried, scratched to get loose, but Cora had stood her ground. For good reason. She worked long hours and had no time for puppies. Not if she wanted to continue visiting the group home and do as much volunteering as she normally did to fill in the empty hours.

But the guilt ate away at her conscience no matter what she told herself. *Christ, not now. Not now when all hell is about to break loose.* Everyone who worked the old case knew the next killing would be happening this week. If the perp stayed true to form, it would be midweek. No doubt, Hunter had arrived when he did because he knew it too.

"Hey, Hunter..." Larry turned and spoke to Kal.

"The name is Agent Hunter or Kal."

"Right. Hunter, have you ever heard a little

puppy make so much noise?"

Catching on to the glint in Larry's eyes, Kal shook his head. "Nope. Figure she had to be heartbroken. Probably never be the same after that terrible rejection."

"Oh, bite me, you two. I can't take care of a puppy with my schedule. Especially now. Let's talk job. You know that the criminal is scheduled to hit someone in the city this coming week, right? I'm thinking Tuesday or Wednesday if he stays true to form."

Larry straightened up, losing his cheeky grin, and nodded. "I agree. He's probably here by now and getting ready to kill his next victim."

Kal added, "You think he plans ahead? See, I don't agree. Or at least, I don't think the original killer did. This guy probably does because he aims for a specific breed, those the law can't nab for one reason or another."

Cora couldn't believe that here was another person who thought as she did. After many arguments to the opposite, she still believed this guy wasn't the same person. She finally let her gaze meet Hunter's. "You think he's a different man?"

"No doubt about it."

Larry piped up, "Yet he uses all the same traditions for his crimes. Every single victim is killed the same way, same weapons, same day. Only one person can know all those aspects of the various cases. He has to be our original guy."

Stubborn, Kal shook his head. "Don't believe so. And I know I'm probably the only dissenter, but something tells me this guy has an agenda whereas the first creep chose random subjects. It's what made him so hard to catch."

Cora smiled, her first in what seemed like forever. It just felt good to have another law enforcement person who recognized what she saw. That the man they were after did have a plan. Now all they needed to do was check into the list of fugitives running free in New Orleans who needed killing. Sadly, there were many around her city who fit that description, they'd never be able to round them all up. She chuckled and noticed the others staring at her.

"Just thinking... we have our work cut out for us if we have to appeal to the scums of our New Orleans' society. They don't take kindly to any form of law enforcement."

The others caught on to her thought direction and both nodded in agreement. Larry added, "No doubt we'll have our hands full. Or, we could just wait and haul in the bodies."

"Like that's going to happen. We wear badges that come with a specific job, whether it leaves a bad taste in our mouth or not." Cora spoke with force. She knew their biggest problem wasn't only in finding the people who hid from the law but giving them protection as they would for any citizen. Not something she looked forward to, but every person alive had the right to protection.

Trying to explain this to a lawbreaker would be a challenge. Who in their right mind would believe a cop had their safety in mind when they wanted to bring them into lockup for their own good?

Larry stood up, his empty coffee cup in his hand as he moved to rinse it and leave it in the sink. "We've got a lot of work to do. I suggest we head to the office, go through the files, and divvy up the criminal element of New Orleans' Eighth District amongst the other detectives. It's going to be a long couple of days, and I for one am not looking forward to the workload."

"Larry, you have other responsibilities and a shitload of officers to do your bidding." Cora cleaned her cup too.

"Yeah, I know. But in the end, I'll be wearing this mess, so I need to stay involved. Bonny will understand."

"If you need a place for her to stay while you're so busy, Mom's got a spare room in her apartment, and you know they get along well. They'll have a ball playing cards while we work our tails off."

"You're right. Think I'll make those arrangements. Thanks, Toots. I worry. Can't help it. Don't know what I'd do if you all didn't help out." Larry stomped into the other part of the house, his phone in his hand.

Cora watched the shock on Hunter's face and had to elaborate. "Bonny's his wife. She has early-onset Alzheimer's and frets when he's gone too long. She starts ahh... crying and it's hell for him to settle her down again. My mom used to be a nurse and has a way with her, so it's the best answer sometimes when work gets in his way."

"Lord, I'm sorry. It must be hell." Kal picked up the other cups, rinsed them all again and set them in the drainer. "For some reason, I thought you two were a thing."

"What? Why in the hell would you think that?"

Hunter looked uncomfortable, but she wouldn't let him off the hook. She really wanted to know what put that bee in his bonnet.

"He walked into the house like he owned it, didn't knock. I don't know. I got the wrong idea from the way he talked to you I guess."

Anger above what the infraction called for slammed into Cora, and she blasted him. "Well clear that shit outta your head. We're colleagues and old buddies, nothing else."

"Right. Cleared. Sorry."

Chapter Eleven

Kal couldn't believe a woman could turn so quickly. One minute she was grinning, laughing at the ridiculous, and the next, pissed at him for taking something logical for granted. Although now that he thought about it, the idea had entered his head a long time ago when Larry had stuck up for this rookie so vehemently. He should have suspected something when they caught her in a wedding dress. Mind you, he'd found out the circumstances for why she was wearing it, but still, he hadn't read the room very well.

Thinking about his first view of the woman after ten years had him grinning. God, what a picture she made! All white satin ruffles and lace, torn sleeves, bare feet, messed up makeup, a goofy smile on her face, and puppies all over her flared out skirts. He'd never forget the image. Whenever he needed to lighten up and feel soft, he now had a memory to revisit that would instantly soothe him.

Suddenly, he noticed her silence and realized he had taken the washcloth and was wiping the sink and counter. Feeling stupid, he dropped the offending cloth and stuck his hands in his pockets. "What's next?"

Grinning at his discomfort, yet saying nothing, Cora changed the subject. "Now we head into the office, check the files for the most recent Badass list, and start rounding them up. If they refuse our protection, we give them a warning and make them understand they need to watch their backs or get a bodyguard. It's serious."

"Can't wait." He returned her grin and felt a moment of complete togetherness, kind of like he used to experience with Shawn. "I have another guy on my team, Agent Fred Falkner. He's a young genius with his laptop, not much use for any street work, but he'll guide us anywhere, anytime. I left him at the hotel to settle in. Maybe you'd have a spot he could work from in your office."

"Since I doubt I'll be spending much time there over the next few days, he can use my desk."

Once they'd organized their next moves, Kal drove back to the headquarters with Cora in her jeep, while Larry headed home to make arrangements for his wife. Clinging to the open frame as he settled in, Kal pointed at the veil still tied around the steering wheel. "You must have gotten a few stares driving around with this blowing in the wind."

"You wouldn't believe me if I told you all the trouble it brought me, from numerous catcalls to being rear-ended by a young idiot wanting a photo." She pulled the offending material off the wheel, rolled it up, and stuffed it under the seat.

"Hey. Wait. It'll get dirty there. Don't you have somewhere else you can put it?"

"Sure, up your ass if you don't keep your unwanted comments to yourself."

Kal's startled look had her glaring his way until he began to laugh. Then her face stopped bristling, and she chuckled too. "Sorry. I'm still kind of gnarly over that whole debacle. My friend Sadie planned her wedding for over a year. Every detail, and I mean down to what pickles they'd be using for the hors d'oeuvres. Go figure, she finds out minutes before the ceremony her fiancé is a cheating prick and will be fathering her partner's baby. I mean, that kind of nonsense only happens in movies, right? Not real life."

Kal forced his face not to divulge the shock he felt at her words. How could anyone be so cruel? He didn't understand it himself. As much as he'd never found the woman he needed to make his life whole, he wouldn't hurt another person so horribly, break their hearts, and weasel out of the mess by being a coward. "Your friend... she took off?"

"Yep. Made me swap clothes with her, hightailed it to the airport, and used the tickets they'd bought for their honeymoon. By now, she should be on board the cruise they'd planned together. I hope she doesn't spend the whole time crying over the past. Poor baby, she really thought they'd have one of those happy-ever-after romance endings."

"Don't scoff, there are a few out there. My parents had that kind of relationship before the end."

"The end. What happened?"

"He found a younger woman and left Mom."

Cora let out a squeal. "Seriously? You mean to tell me—"

Kal laughed and held up his hand. "Sorry. Just messin' with you. My dad's gone, but Mom is fine. She brought me up as a single mom and still lives in the same apartment they had back then."

"You're a cruel bastard, you are. And quit laughing. It's actually what happened to my folks, so I'm rather sensitive to that kind of thing."

Now Kal felt like a real jackass. "God, Cora, I'm sorry. I would never have teased if I'd known... hold it. Why are you laughing?"

"Gotcha! Just so you know, two can play at that game, dude." She stopped the jeep in front of a huge building with a wraparound veranda that looked more like a mansion than a police station.

"Where are we?"

"It's the home where my mom lives. Look, she frets... hell they all do. I need to let them see for themselves that I'm fine after these last few days. It's a daughter duty thing."

Kal shook his head, not sure why he was grinning. Something in the discomfort she couldn't hide made him know that her embarrassment over having people worry about her came in second to her responsibility to let them know she cared about their feelings.

"No problem. I'm happy to see the inside of a retirement home. Planning on residing in one myself in say... fifty or sixty years."

"Yeah, well while you're there you can go screw yourself. And wipe that silly grin off your face. Look, I'll only be a minute."

"No need. Looks like they saw your jeep and are coming to you."

Sure enough, a woman who looked enough like Cora to be her mother and three other retirees that were together had spotted her and were trudging her way. Wanting to stop them from reaching the vehicle, she jumped out and curtailed their invasion. "I'm fine. You can go back inside and play cards or get started on whatever mischief you're up to this morning."

"You know very well, it's our stitch and bitch morning." One of the women, slim and a looker, came right up to Cora, relief evident in the look of pride on her face. The way she wrapped an arm around the blonde's shoulder and patted her back lovingly, her reaction made Kal figure her to be

Cora's mother.

"Good. No doubt, you'll be bitching about me all morning. Gotta go."

Her mother turned to Kal who'd stepped from the jeep and approached as politeness dictated. "Hello."

"Ma'am."

Without turning away from him, she asked Cora, "Who's the McStunning dude, honey?"

Kal laughed and winked at Cora, surprisingly anxious to hear her reply.

"A drone from New York, Special Agent Kal Hunter. Now back off and let us get to work. These next few days will be busy, so don't expect me to be around, and don't worry or call every few hours. No texts either. I mean it, Mom." She pointed meaningfully at the other woman and then yelled to the group of fellows on the veranda who had been listening to their conversation. "That means you guys too, right? I'll be needing to concentrate, so deal with your own squabbles, okay?"

Various agreements sounded and Kal could tell by the way they answered, Cora meant a lot to every one of these old people. It warmed his heart to see such a degree of interaction between the young detective and the older residents.

Cora extricated herself from her mother's arms and the others who needed to share their love and headed back to the vehicle, calling, "Come on, lover boy. They'll keep you here all day if you don't escape now."

On the road again, Cora yelled over the noise of her blaring radio. "Don't say a word. If I didn't let them see me for themselves, they'd storm the station."

Kal lifted his hands to ward off her pissiness. Shaking his head innocently, he said, "It's nice. You're lucky." When he saw the scowl, he leaned back and added, "Shutting up now."

Looking everywhere but at him, she sped up, forcing him to grab the handle and turn away so she wouldn't see his eyes closed and the dread on his face. A few minutes later she whipped into a parking place filled with cars and wheeled into the slot where the sign read Detective Taylor. Before they made it inside the building, a uniformed officer approached, his face red and sweaty, his eyes full of worry. "Cora, can I have a moment?"

Cora stopped, looked at him, and reached out her hand. "Sure, Miguel." Once they shook, she turned to Kal who'd stepped up behind her.

"Officer Miguel Salida meet Special Agent Hunter. He's working with us on an old case from New York." She waited for the men to shake hands, looked at Miguel, and added, "Something up?"

"My mom, she's worse. They took her from the Home to the hospital. She calls for you, says she needs to tell you something... no one else. Jesus, I know you're busy, but it would mean a lot if you could stop by and see her when you get a chance. Ease her mind while she's in such pain."

"She's worse? I'm so sorry, bro. Of course, I'll stop... make it a priority. I have to zip into the office to get some printouts, and then I'll go to her."

Miguel's face softened. "You've been ridiculously kind to her. She loves you as much as the rest of our family. I can never repay you, mi hermana."

"Hey, don't get all sentimental on me, Miguel. Today isn't the day you wanna go there. After the weekend I just passed, I might end up slobbering all over you."

A twinkle appeared in Miguel's eye, but he pretended to zip his mouth and hide his grin. "Gracias, Cora. Hasta luego."

Kal stood aside and kept his mouth shut. It had been illuminating for him to see the cussing woman with the hard-assed attitude be approached and treat her obvious rookie with such kindness. He liked it... liked her better for it.

Until she caught his soft smile and growled the words, "Wipe that silly smirk off your face, Hunter. We have a lot of work to do."

Chapter Twelve

The list was too bloody long.

Kal knew they had criminals living in the district, but once they showed on paper, he had to accept they had their work cut out for them for the next few days. The inventory held names from only the immediate area, which didn't even take into account all the other regions in New Orleans.

"Son of a bitch, look at how many lowlifes we have to contact."

Not wanting her to feel bad, Kal admitted, "No worse than most major cities."

"Undoubtedly, but first, I have to make a stop."

He knew she'd follow up on her promise. Not surprising, her next statement showed him to be right.

"I'm off to the hospital, Hunter. You can come with me or work from the office and get more info about the top idiots on this list. We can meet later."

Kal felt offended. His partner had arrived, and following Kal's text that Cora had offered her desk for him to work from, was now comfortably installed at it. "Freddie here will keep us up to date with the facts we need. I'd rather stick with you and start working on these names as soon as possible."

He wasn't overwhelmed by the noise or numerous desks, monitors, officers both in uniform and in plain clothes all sporting badges, but he preferred to be on the street with her... protecting her. Always at the back of his mind, he remembered that only one person had ever caught up with the demented bastard ten years ago. And the person who'd wavered was fortunate to be alive.

She'd almost stopped him, had battled with him, and then froze. Rather than using the rifle he'd retrieved; the assassin had heard them coming and ran off. If they were wrong, and it was the original cold-case killer back in action, wouldn't she be first on his hit-list for New Orleans?

The desire to finish off the person who'd been that close could be paramount. It made sense. Even though the killer now seemed to be after the bad guys, he might still hold a grievance against this woman. And the thought jabbed his head like stabs of pain that couldn't be shaken loose.

Cora edged closer to the thin, curly-headed man she'd just met, the eager young agent who appeared to idolize his partner. "That okay with you, Agent

Falkner?"

"It's Fred, ma'am." His shyness was appealing.

Shocked that she'd bother checking with his partner, it made Kal feel ashamed of his low expectation of Freddie and his way of taking him for granted. He'd never accepted him in the role as his real sidekick and had flipped him off to looking after hated office details while he went about his business alone.

Jesus, had he been a jerk with the kid? *He's not a kid...* the thought popped into his head, and he took a second look at the guy who'd all but turned inside out to be accepted. The tall, gangly man with the thatch of dark curly hair, wearing glasses over green eyes that didn't miss much stared back.

Feeling ashamed, realizing he'd been at fault, he waited to see what Freddie had to say. First, he looked at Kal for some sort of guidance and then back to Cora. "I'll hang in here and keep the information flowing. We still need to get addresses for a lot of these names, and I'm thinking I'll bring up all the FBI databases that might give me the answers, then surf the web and even check into social media. It's amazing the junk people throw out there thinking it can't be retrieved."

"Hell, use driver's licenses, phone companies or any other public venue you can think of. We need to contact them asap. Some, I already know where to find, but the one's I ticked for you are off the grid, even with the snitches we use. So, any data you come up with will be a help."

"Okay, it's settled, but thanks for asking." He checked Kal as if to see whether he'd made the right choice.

Instinctively, Kal reached out. He stepped closer and touched Freddie's arm briefly, looked him in the eye and answered, "Appreciate this, bro. I've bragged to Cora about how valuable you are on your laptop. Now she'll get to see for herself."

Suddenly, Kal felt a wet nose in his hand and turned to see two black eyes peering at him from under Freddie's desk.

"Sam?"

The answering whine couldn't be ignored. Kal's look drilled into Fred. "Seriously, you brought the dog?"

Fred fiddled with the pen in his hand and cleared his throat. "After you left, the kennel called the office and said he wouldn't settle. That he was upsetting the other dogs so much, he couldn't stay."

"Christ, that's their business." Frustration rang in Kal's voice and Sam reacted. He laid his furry long nose on Kal's shoe and cried piteously.

"All I know is they tried approaching to give him a sedative, but no such luck. He scared the pants off all three workers. They demanded you fetch him. I had no choice."

"Sam!" Kal pointed at the dog who tried to back into his hiding place. "How could you?"

Sam howled.

"Stop it."

Instant silence followed, other than Cora's snickering.

Kal turned his flushed face to his partner. "You should have called me."

"Yeah, I guess. Except I had a plane to catch. It was either bring him with me or stay back myself. Had no choice. The hotel gave me permission to have the animal in our room so..."

"So, you took the easy way. Except he wouldn't stay in the room, would he?"

"Nope. He smelled you everywhere and paced from the time we arrived, crying piteously. Man, seriously, he broke my heart. I couldn't leave him behind making all that noise."

"Well, he's staying with you now. You brought him, he's you're responsibility."

Kal shushed the demanding dog and tried not to see the glee Cora didn't hide when she stopped pretending to go through her emails on her phone and watched the animal now glued to his leg.

She chuckled. "People say folks purposely choose the breed that looks most like them."

Fred bit off a laugh and covered his mouth.

Asshole partner did have a sense of humor after all. Kal knew what Sam looked like to others. Ugly, oversized, a mix of so many colors, one couldn't say if he were black, brown, orange, or just plain mud. Most people turned away with derision when they saw the animal. Was he the only one who noticed the intelligence in the canine's eerie blue eyes and felt the complete adoration his pet extended?

Cora stepped closer, reached out her hand, and waited until the dog sniffed it. Except he didn't. Sniff it. He hid his head behind Kal's leg as if shyness refused to let him act normal. It was so obvious, Cora giggled and didn't force the issue. "I do believe your pet is shy, Hunter."

"He's not used to women. Doesn't like strangers. Hell, I don't know why he acts so timid. He isn't when we're alone. Freddie, he stays with you."

"Sure. No problem."

"Keep in touch, right?"

Glowing, Freddie nodded. "Yep. You'll be getting texts as soon as I have anything. Catch up with you later."

"You bet."

Cora headed toward the exit, and he followed, unable to keep his eyes off the way her body moved.

Built strong, slender and in perfect proportion, he'd never seen a woman walk with such incredible movements that weren't quite a wiggle, but every part flowed perfectly. As if each slithered step had been practiced... eye-catching to any full-blooded male.

He swallowed and turned to see three other men sitting at their desks with their eyes glued to the same butt he'd just looked away from. Guess he

wasn't the only one captivated by this detective.
What he didn't see was Sam close behind him.

Chapter Thirteen

Cora repeated her words to a furious Kal yet again. "Look, it's no biggie taking him along. Hell, it's just a jeep. There's room in the back. I figured Sam'd be happier in the open vehicle rather than the police SUV. It's against the law to leave an animal closed in with these temperatures."

Kal, arms crossed, still refused to soften to Sam. "He disobeyed my hand signal back in the office. We've worked on those same tricks for months, and Sam never ignores my commands. Not like he did today."

"Give him a break. It's a different place, and he's surrounded by strangers."

Sensing he was in a big can of shit by the low whine of begging that never stopped until finally Kal couldn't take the stare from an incredulous Cora anymore. She'd tried soothing the upset animal with her kind words. "It's okay, buddy.

You're welcome in my car anytime." But they'd had no effect.

The pitiful whines stopped for a few seconds as he'd listened, but then he'd turned his face away to lay it on the top of Kal's head, showing where his true allegiance lay. Kal tried pushing him away, and it worked for a few seconds, but the dog had the back seat and couldn't be reached easily. Within seconds, the snout returned to nestle on Kal's hair.

"Stop it, Sam. You're slobbering all over me. I mean it."

The dog seemed thrilled to be addressed finally by his master. He licked the side of Kal's face feverishly in his excitement.

"Okay, okay. You're forgiven. But next time I give you an order, you obey. I mean it. Or I'll sell you to a meat-packing plant."

The dog actually opened his mouth and made a sound of derision, while a smile lit up his ugly mug.

Cora, watching in the rearview mirror, broke out laughing. "Seriously, you two are a pair. He's got your number. Bet he shares your bed."

"Not because he's invited. Bloody animal sneaks in there after he knows I'm asleep."

Driving as usual, like she's out to win a race, Cora sneered. "Sure, it's not your fault. Ever hear of closing a door."

Kal's satisfied sniff came before his answer. "Yes, ma'am. Fact is… the beast can open any doorhandle invented. Gave up after the third one I installed."

Laughter rang out over the booming music Kal had turned down to a dull roar. Cora pulled into the hospital parking area and found a place in the shade.

"You should find a vending machine in the lobby and get him some water. There's probably an old take-out container you can use in the back. I don't imagine I'll be too long visiting Miguel's mom."

***

Once she'd said her piece, Cora grabbed the side rail to exit and felt her hand gently licked before she sauntered off to disappear through the main doors.

This time she knew better than to fondle the dog. Acceptance had to be on his terms. She got it. Not her problem. She had her own crap to worry about. After reading the numerous texts from Mona that followed her since she separated that morning, she couldn't decide what the hell to do.

It seems the blasted pup who'd made up her mind Cora belonged to her had carried on like a heartbroken little shit. Now what the hell was that all about? She had no time to deal with Mona's problems. They'd have to wait.

Chapter Fourteen

Kal bought a half dozen bottles of water, three for Sam, one for cleaning out a dish, and the rest for him and Cora. Then he'd gone through the ridiculous mess in the back of her Jeep and found more old bowls than he imagined. Thankfully, the food had been eaten, but who kept dried-up old plastic containers?

Cleaning out the chaos, he found a garbage can to rid the vehicle of most of the debris and washed the one he used for Sam. Not caring about total cleanliness, Sam pushed and wriggled around him until he finally gave up and filled the small Chinese-food basin with water. Then he downed a bottle himself.

Finding an old rope amongst the rest of the junk, he used it to tie Sam inside the Jeep and gave him the order to stay. Once he knew that Sam would do so, he tracked Cora into the hospital.

It had bothered him letting her out if his sight. Not that he felt they'd been followed, he'd checked to be sure, but one never knew where trouble lay waiting.

Flashing his badge, he checked the room number for Mrs. Salida, obeyed directions, and hearing voices, he stood near the door rather than interrupting.

Cora kept her tone low, but the sick woman spoke louder, and he had no trouble hearing words that shocked. She'd kept this to herself all these years. No wonder she needed to clear her conscience before she met her maker.

***

Stunned, Cora hadn't expected the deterioration noticeable in the earlier robust woman who'd lived down the hall from her mother in the Home. Now, Mrs. Salida's cheeks were shrunken, her color appearing gray and the film over her eyes left Cora in no doubt. She only had a short time left in this world.

Compassion for the poor woman rose, and she had to control it. She didn't want to let her concern show in case it put fear into the sickly old dear.

Reaching for the hand that seemed to be searching, she held it gently and took the closest seat next to the patient.

"Cora? Honey? Is that you?"

"Yes, Mrs. Salida. It's me. Miguel spoke to me this morning, saying you wanted to talk with me. I came as soon as I could."

First, the woman coughed, and Cora had to lift her shoulders to help her control the wheezing that followed. Finally, after a bit of water, Mrs. Salida began to speak in earnest. Cracking, like a pipe not in use for a long time, her voice built from a low pitch to where she almost hollered the words, forcing them out.

"I've waited too long to share my story. But it needs to be told. One night, ten years ago, my son Sergio and I had a terrible fight over his drug dependency. I was filled with rage. For the first time in his life, I-I slapped him."

Emotion created more coughing, and the nurse came in to administer a pill and use a puffer to help clear the passageway so Mrs. Salida could continue her story. Once she left the room, the old woman resumed. "My boy was a mess, emotionally wasted, needing a fix. He wouldn't let me take him to the hospital. He wanted me to give him money. I had none. He begged me first... then he got angry and pushed me."

Cora felt a stranglehold on her hand as the woman leaned forward to put emphasis on her words. "Do you know what it's like to say no to your sick son, living in hell?"

Cora shook her head. "I'm sorry. I don't have any children. I can't even imagine."

"I blame myself. For what happened. He stormed from the house and ran into the woods. I followed him." Mrs. Salida began to cry, making it harder to understand her words.

Wanting to give her time to recuperate, Cora queried, "Mrs. Salida, would it be okay for me to record this conversation... my memory isn't what it used to be."

"You do what you think best. I can't protect my family any longer."

"Thank you. I know Miguel would be proud of you for coming forward and sharing your story. Okay, can you tell me what happened next?"

"A man ran past. I thought it was my Sergio. I almost approached. Until I saw him throw something into the bushes. He looked at his chest and then tore off his gray sweatshirt. Once the hood left his face, I knew it wasn't my son. The poor soul crouched and wailed low like a demented fiend not wanting attention. I swear the hair rose all over my body. Fear made my stomach heave. It was terrible." Her hand tightened on Cora's in memory of her reaction. "As I prayed, I swallowed over and over to stop from making any noise. I've never seen anyone in such anguish."

As the memory of her fear resurfaced, Cora saw a change come over the sick woman. Her hands began to thrash as if pushing away something too horrible to see. Leaning over, she gently gathered the flailing hands again and rubbed their backs soothingly. "Shush now, darling. It's okay. You can tell Cora your story, and then let it go. It's too much for you to carry with you."

Cora's interest had spiked at the vivid mind-picture of a man wearing a hoodie who ran off into the woods. Could it possibly be the same man she'd fought with? She'd always believed he'd gone in a different direction; they'd all searched the other side of the hill from where Mrs. Salida and her sons lived.

But he could have doubled back. Goddamn, the ghost who'd haunted her nights for so long had been intelligent, no one denied that.

As if waking from a nightmare, Mrs. Salida's eyes flew open, and she blindly jerked forward. "Cora?"

"I'm still here. Take your time, honey. I won't leave you until you've had your say. I promise. Last thing you told me was about another man in the woods. Did you find Sergio too?"

"I did. But we didn't speak. I couldn't move. The devil fled. It seemed as if he'd come to a decision because he talked to himself."

"Could you hear what he said?"

"Yes. He kept repeating, growling words that sounded like no more... no more. Ever. Never. No more."

"Then what happened?"

"He ran away. He never saw me behind the rock. Neither did Sergio who suddenly appeared at the place where the man had been crouching. He picked up what looked like a stick in the dark to examine it. I remember, he put on the sweater and had the hood pulled over his face. Then he disappeared. I think I closed my eyes to pray that I could find the right words that would bring him home with me. But I never got to speak."

"How sad for you. I'm so sorry."

"Me too. Until the next day when I saw the news where a family outside those very woods had been killed, shot with a rifle. That's when I knew. Sergio had picked up a gun, not a stick."

"What are you saying, Mrs. Salida?" Cora needed to hear the words from the woman's own mouth.

Swallowing now, as if her mouth were dry, Mrs. Salida tried to force those last words from her parched throat.

Seeing her distress, Cora held the straw from the water glass to her lips and waited until the woman had a few sips. Pity overwhelming her, she added, "You don't need to say anything else."

"Yes. I do. My Sergio had money that night, enough to buy his overdose. I found him dead in the morning on the steps outside my back door. He had a broken piggy bank lying next to him. Before I called the police, I hid it in my night table. God help me, I think it belonged to the family he shot when he stole from them."

Suddenly, the distraught woman grabbed onto Cora's arm so she could pull herself upright. She stared at Cora, her eyes filled with grief and guilt.

"I never meant to withhold evidence, Cora. I was protecting my son, my family. And my own guilt for turning Sergio away from his mama with a slap to remember her by. God forgive me, I prayed every day for those poor people."

"It's not your sin, Mrs. Salida. And Sergio paid for his. Rest now, darling."

The old woman's eyes drilled into Cora's. Her forgiveness seemed to push out Mrs. Salida's sorrow and a smile appeared.

"I'm fine now, baby. Go. Be happy. Tell Miguel I love him."

Those were the last words spoken before the lady sunk into a coma-like sleep, finally at peace.

Chapter Fifteen

Cora sat back in her chair, digesting the words she'd just heard. My God! All these years later, they find out that the real killer of that poor unsuspecting family had been a pitiful druggie, looking for money for his next fix. Lordy, what a sad world when someone is driven to the length he'd go to for money to relieve his pain and give him his next high.

Within seconds, she felt the presence of another in the room behind her. How she knew it was him seemed inconceivable, but she wasn't wrong. He moved closer and crouched next to the chair, reaching to touch her arm.

"I heard most of what she said. We can finally put our particular theory to rest and accept the truth."

She looked into his face to see the brilliant green of his eyes filled with concern. She yanked her arm away and bristled. "Don't know what you mean." She shot to her feet and moved to the corridor.

In seconds, he caught up to her, stood behind, and spoke with conviction. "I always believed that our cold-case killer had finished that night with the deaths of four more people beside that unfortunate store clerk. We knew he'd taken the rifle. What else were we to think? Now we know different."

Cora wouldn't turn, wouldn't let him see her face, see the tears of relief that came straight from her stricken heart. A heart that had been filled with self-loathing for so long, it wouldn't release that loathing easily.

"It's over." She muffled the words, wriggled from his presence, and tried to walk away. He wouldn't let her. Arms came around her from behind and held her tight.

God help me, how did he know I'd need to be held? Nothing had ever felt so perfect. His strength oozed into her as if by osmosis it could blend with hers and keep her upright. She needed this, needed to feel the relief she'd never thought would ever be possible.

It hadn't been her fault that the family had died. Not pulling the trigger that night had nothing to do with their deaths. *God, help me, I'm so thankful the tragedy hadn't happened because I froze.* Not knowing if she suffered a sick kind of reaction, or the way any sane person would feel, but the overwhelming thankfulness made her knees weak and kept the tears flowing.

Trying to escape, go to a washroom, hide her shameful display, she again wriggled to jerk free. Yet again he held her close. This time his chin rested on her shoulder as he whispered in her ear, "It's okay. I understand. You can take a minute, and I'll just hold on. I need to."

He seemed to ramble as if he couldn't stop and it dawned on her that maybe he had carried some of the guilt from that night too. Closing her eyes, she stopped struggling and leaned back against him. Her mind returned to the house where he'd again used his body, his strong arms trying to protect her from the horror that awaited after the gunshots had been reported. After they'd followed what they thought was the killer's trail.

He'd held her close, trying to stop her from seeing the unforgettable. The picture that had haunted her for many nights to come until after she'd worked it out with her conscience. The deal included her suffering one weekend a year in order to have some sort of peace the rest of the nights. It took time, but eventually it worked. She'd found a strange kind of resolution, some might call it compromise within herself, one she could live with.

Whether right or wrong, she'd made up for that sad night by working her ass off and becoming a cop many admired, and others were scared to push. Her record kept advancing with cases solved.

But no matter how hard she worked, or how many wins she racked up, when she looked into the mirror, she'd see that same pitiful girl with her long tied-back hair, her big revealing swollen eyes, and a mouth that wouldn't stop trembling.

Such a child!

So filled with romantic ideals.

An idiot who'd wanted to make her dad proud and save the world.

What crap!

She swallowed the ridiculous lump of emotion. Maybe now she could look in a mirror and see the real woman. A flawed individual trying her hardest. A huge sigh gathered. She released it and felt his arms tighten. The time had come to let go of the past.

Could she? Until she heard his words, she wasn't sure.

"You're a nice person, Cora. A good cop. And a sweetheart for taking the time you did for Mrs. Salida."

She listened to his warm voice. Heartfelt, knowing the truth, she admitted, "I'm glad you were here." Swallowing the rising sob, this time when she forced herself out of his arms, he let her go. She didn't look at him, just headed straight to the washroom to check if the mirror would finally let her see the woman she was today and not the terrified girl from ten years ago.

Chapter Sixteen

Kal still felt shaky. It's what Cora did to him. Could she sense his predicament? His need to hold her when she'd been on the edge? She'd seemed so filled with emotion that he felt worry eating away at his macho image. No man wants to come off as being a pussy or susceptible to weakness. At least, he sure as hell didn't. No cop worth his salt wanted to appear pathetic.

Why she twisted his insides, he'd never know? It had happened before, his need to protect her. Time to stop that foolishness before she cottoned on to the weirdness he couldn't seem to control.

He went to the men's room, threw cold water on his face, and washed his hands. Damn heat. The Big Easy never gave an inch. Even the hospital's air conditioning didn't register. But it was as good an excuse as any for the damp eyes and inside tremors.

Time to get to the jeep... and more than time

to get to work. He didn't want to think about the sensations that had exploded when he'd held Cora. How sweet it felt, how right...

Once he stepped outside the main doors, he heard the racket before he'd walked ten steps.

Sam!?

Jesus, couldn't he leave that animal alone for five minutes without this nonsense?

He hurried to where they'd left the jeep and saw that not only had his dog gotten loose, with a rope trailing, he'd attacked a man, forcing him against the door of a truck. Fangs glistening, his warning growls were deadly serious.

"What the hell is going on? Sam, lay off."

Sam stepped back a little and laid down, his eyes never leaving the now sagging man whose hands were swiping at his glistening face and dripping neck.

When the fellow tried to move forward, Sam's threatening snarls left them all in no uncertainty that it wasn't happening until Kal said it could.

Before the words formed, Cora approached and started to laugh. "You back at your old tricks, Marley? Breaking into vehicles, looking for change?"

"Nope, not me Miss Cora. I'm walking along, minding my own business when this here vicious beast attacked me."

"Sure, you were." Suddenly they all watched as Sam went over to a tool that lay on the ground, almost hidden by the truck's bumper and lifted it into his mouth. He brought it to Kal and dropped it in front of him. Then he turned back to the fidgety criminal and showed his teeth once again, a rumble sounded as if to say that's bullshit and you know it.

Cora leaned over to pick it up. She lifted the iron rod to show Marley. "This yours?"

"Never saw it before in my life."

"Yeah? Ever heard of fingerprints, Marley? We have yours on file in the database, right?"

Marley, knowing the game was up, deflated. "I haven't eaten since yesterday, Miss Cora. I swear it on my daddy's grave."

"You hated your daddy. You need a drink, is what you need."

A shifty look appeared, and Marley moved from one foot to another. "It's a family curse. You know that."

"I also know you see a hell of a lot of what happens on the streets, my old friend." She held out a folded paper. "If you can give me the whereabouts of some of the names on this list, I might be able to get Agent Hunter to call off his K-Nine attack dog before he rips your throat open."

Chapter Seventeen

Armed with the scrawled-on list, Kal sat next to Cora as she drove in her normal aggressive fashion. "That's some mean animal you have there, Hunter. He's been trained."

"Can't say he has or hasn't. I only found him early this year. He followed me home one night."

"Why?"

"What do you mean why?"

"You must have done something to make him trust you."

"Nah. Not really. I'd pulled into a Subway and bought a sandwich. He caught up to me as I was sitting on the table outside scoffing it down like I was starving, because I was. We were working a tough case, hadn't stopped to eat anything all day, and it was now midnight. He kind of appeared out of nowhere, looking scruffy as hell, beaten and bruised, much meaner than this fatter version, and obviously hungry."

Kal remembered that night. He'd sat on the table so he could put his feet on the bench as the ground was still mucky from the earlier rain. Fastidious, he worried about the new shoes he'd paid too much money for. Out of nowhere, a face appeared in front of him. A face that would scare the pants off any sane person if he hadn't been wearing a firearm and knew how to use it.

What looked like a canine in the dark, stepped forward so the light proved his assumptions were correct. It was a dog. The ugliest looking brute he'd ever seen. Huge, barrel-like around its starving narrow girth, long legs that seemed to wobble, he sat in front of Kal. Pride shone from hungry blue eyes. One ear flopped over as if it had given up the fight while the other stood at attention. He didn't beg, but his manner left Kal no delusions that this animal needed to eat.

As hungry as he was, something told him the poor, weakened stray needed food more. Tearing pieces off the foot-long, meat-filled sandwich he'd splurged on, he dropped them on the clean bench and waited for the dog to snatch at them.

Only that's not what happened. Instead, the starving animal carefully reached for each piece and chewed it fastidiously. Kal had never seen anything like it. He related to the monster instantly. It was how he ate, no matter how hungry he became. What started as a gesture of friendliness ended with him being followed.

Without his knowing it would happen, he'd gotten to his vehicle, opened the door to say his goodbyes to the stalker, and found the beast had streaked into his car with no intentions of leaving.

No matter how he begged, or ranted, or even swung his gun threateningly – the one portion of the evening he wasn't proud of and later using his extreme lack of sleep and tough assignment overload as his excuse – nothing worked. Finally, knowing he needed his bed, he'd just gotten in the car, drove home, and as he got out of the SUV, so did the stubborn monster.

Eventually worn down, he'd left Sam outside only to find him still there the next morning. That night, the dog waited, and this time when Kal opened the door, the animal brushed past him, leapt onto the couch, and his eyes dared Kal to do something. Instantly, Kal made up his mind to set some rules. He'd pointed at his favorite easy chair and grouched, "This is my seat. Got it?"

Sam's intelligence couldn't be doubted when he'd looked at Kal, then the chair, flattened his ear, and growled gently. That was the end of the story. The ridiculous shadow had never left. Feeling like an adoptee rather than the other way around, he noticed that Cora was still waiting for his story.

"If you promise you won't laugh, one day I'll tell you how we met."

"Deal." Her hand reached forward and pressed

where it read "office phone" in her vehicle's built-in screen.

In minutes, the ringing changed to an answer. "Hey, Detective, what's up?"

"Addy, I need you to check something and get back to me asap."

"Sure. What do you need?"

"Can you go into the files of that still-open cold-case from ten years ago that I left on my desk? Last victims were Leroy Fetner, store clerk, and the Adamsons, family of four. I need to know if there was ever anything found missing from the Adamson's home?"

"Okay. I'm on it. I'll get back to you."

Cora turned to Kal. "Even though I believe Mrs. Salida, I need to know if they have the piggybank listed. It would be the final link, and we would be able to put the case to bed."

Before he could answer, the phone rang, and she reached out. "Addy, did you find anything?"

"Nope. That was another reason they assumed it was the killer who'd taken more victims, remember. Nothing had been stolen or vandalized according to what's listed in the computer files."

"Except, he'd left the rifle. He'd never given up his weapon before."

"True, but it was clean of prints and no sign of his last killing, so maybe he screwed up because of mental trauma. And... no money was missing, which made us rule out a burglary gone bad."

"Nothing reported missing. Mr. Adamson still had his wallet. And Mrs. Adamson still wore her jewelry. Nothing looked disturbed according to her family that lived close by."

"Right, I remember now. Okay, thanks."

Kal knew where her mind shifted as if she couldn't believe the earlier evidence from Mrs. Salida that would let her release the guilt she'd worn for so long. He had no intention of letting her get away with it. "Look, according to Mrs. Salida, her son grabbed a piggy bank. Maybe it was new, so the other family or neighbors didn't notice it missing. Obviously, it had money. We'll go and pick it up from Mrs. Salida's night table and it might give us some clues as to where it came from. Maybe there'll still be prints on it. We can trace them to her son. Don't let the doubts mess up your mind. That case is solved."

"Right. You're right. I'll let Miguel hear the tape and ask him to get the piggybank into an evidence bag and bring it in. Right now, we need to start working that list. Marley helped with a few directions. But as far as the first name on the list, I already knew his address. We'll pay him a visit and pass on the warning."

"What's this man done?"

"Nolan Hutchinson II? He's a portfolio manager of nothing better than a huge Ponzi scheme. He's robbing a lot of people out of their life savings and is getting away with millions. Unfortunately, we don't have enough evidence to make an arrest. People give him their money willingly. Recently, he moved somewhere out to the suburbs, put a security system around his place that equals Fort Knox, and only lets his lawyers talk for him in public."

"So why don't we pass on the warning to his lawyers and tick him off as done?"

"Because I like to rattle his chain every so often, let him know we're still waiting for him to fuck up in order to put him away where he deserves to be."

Suddenly, she pulled off the highway into a rich neighborhood of fancy homes and large estates. Pulling over to a classy scrolled, black iron gate with a voice mechanism, she pushed the button and leaned on her door. A male voice lit up the window. "Can I help you?"

"Is Mr. Hutchinson home? If so, I need to speak to him. Tell him Detective Taylor and Special Agent Hunter are here to see him." Cora flashed her badge against the glass, and they heard an abrupt reaction to having a screen filled unexpectedly.

"What's it about?"

"None of your business." Cora turned to Kal and shrugged.

"Fine. I'll tell him you're here."

"Appreciate it."

They heard the click and in just seconds, the voice returned. "He wants to know why you're here."

"Tell him we have a legal issue to talk over and it's for his own safety."

"Wait."

"Ever heard the word please, asshole?"

"You rang our bell."

"That I did and if he doesn't answer me soon, we'll drive away, and he'll never know why he's in danger."

The gate clicked and slowly opened. Another armed guard on that side of the wall waved them to continue up the circular drive. When they stopped in front of the huge front door, Kal appreciated the detail that went into the heavy carved wooden entrance. Everything about the property, from the groomed lawns, the opulent white plantation-looking structure, and the professional landscaping, screamed money.

He followed Cora from the vehicle, giving Sam, again tied to the roof, the order to stay and guard. The animal sat back; his head turned away as if he heard the order but was making no promises.

Cora chuckled at the interaction and then walked up the wide steps between the pillars to the front door. Before she could ring a bell, it opened. The huge, muscled butler stared at them with disdain. "Yes?"

"Hey buddy, you let us in the entrance to see Nolan Hutchinson. I assume he's here and was agreeable to having this visit."

"He is. Follow me." His attitude reminded Kal of a swelled-headed bodyguard he'd known in the past. One who'd earned a life sentence for killing the man he supposedly worked for. Following Cora, he wasn't surprised at her question, "You got a concealed-carry license for that gun?"

"Of course." The brute didn't miss a beat, and Cora let it go. He wondered if it were just her way to pull rank, let the douchebag know she could ask for proof.

He grinned and stayed close as they approached an outdoor area where the French doors were wide open to highlight the large, turquoise, rectangular-shaped pool backed against a water-wall. Various glass-topped tables with poufy red-flowered chairs were scattered in all directions.

They approached one where a man lay in a flowered bathing suit, a magazine on the table next to the finished martini glass. He negligently looked at them as they approached but made no move to sit up or welcome them. He didn't raise his hands to shake theirs or even offer them a drink. "I know why you're here, Cora, and you needn't have bothered to come all this way."

Chapter Eighteen

Cora had no idea what the thieving genius was talking about. "How could you know why we're here?"

"Thompson told me he was going to the police. He needn't have gone to so much trouble. I paid the money into his account this morning."

"Ah! You're starting to unravel, Nolan. It had to happen sooner or later. All those people you now owe money to are going to come to their senses one day soon, and you'll have to pay for your crimes. In the meantime, I'm not here about that... though you have to know I'm always watching you."

This time Hutchinson reacted and swung his legs around to sit on the edge of his lounger. "What the hell are you here for then?"

"Be nice, Nolan. It's just a courtesy call. This is Special Agent Kal Hunter from New York. We have evidence to suspect you might be in possible danger and so we're here to warn you. There's an executioner on the loose, got a whack of people in New York, and now he's on his way here to New Orleans."

"What do mean an executioner?" He scoffed as he asked his question.

Cora's grin screamed sarcasm. "The crazy fool goes around killing people. No one's yet learned why or how he chooses his victims, which makes finding him much tougher."

"What the hell does that have to do with me?"

"Well, our vigilante has an unexplainable fetish. He only kills those he deems as bad-ass rule-breakers who we can't seem to stop from abusing today's system of laws. You fit that profile perfectly. Therefore, we're here to let you know we can't offer you any kind of protection... unless you're willing to stay in our luxurious barred lodgings until he's either caught or disappears again."

"Christ, like that would ever happen." Nolan chuckled as if Cora had told the best joke he'd heard in a while. "What do you mean, again?"

"Ten years ago, there was a cold-case never closed where the killer chose his victims randomly, killed without mercy, and fled after he'd wiped out a half-dozen of our prominent citizens. We're looking at the same MO again. The difference this time around, we believe he only wants the lawbreakers. Guess he's learned to be discriminating."

Nolan started to laugh. "And you think he might have me as one of his targets? I haven't done anything that isn't legal, Detective. If I had, you'd have been on me faster than a hooker bargaining for cash. No doubt, I'd be arrested and jailed. Right?" Nolan laughed as if he'd been told a great joke. "So, what's this guy look like?"

"We don't know much more than he's of regular height and build or he was ten years ago."

"That describes a lot of people. Haven't you anything else for me to watch for?"

"Yeah, he likes to kill swindlers like you."

"He ain't gonna get the chance. I'm pretty well protected here."

"That's what a few of his other victims believed. They can't say the same anymore, 'cause now they're dead. And their scams are over."

Kal broke in before Cora had a chance to tell the bastard what she thought of a man who lived in luxury off suckers who'd saved all their lives for retirement, only to pass the money to a shyster like him. Thinking about it made her sick.

"Pretty cocky, Mr. Hutchinson. Good. Those are always the crooks who hit bottom the hardest. The one's who believe they'll be able to manage the weak believers forever. Think of Mr. Thompson, pal. He's only the beginning in a long line of those who'll soon be after you all the time, people who want what you promised them. Life's not going to be so sweet then."

Nolan shot to his feet and almost fell over. He'd obviously had more than one drink from the empty glass. "Foster, show these people out. They said what they came for. We have nothing further to discuss."

Cora started to leave but hesitated long enough to add, "Thanks for your time, Hutchinson or should I say, Abe Kowalski. I can see that you have a heavy workday. I'm sorry we felt compelled to bother you. Just so you know, you were on the top of our list."

After dropping that bombshell, Cora headed past Foster and straight for the jeep where Sam warmed her seat, completely on guard, his rope coiled on the floor in the back.

Chapter Nineteen

Kal couldn't believe his dog had broken loose from his knots, especially after his implicit instructions. Trust his so-called best friend to pull this stunt today. It sure as hell wasn't the first time, but the aggravation still rankled. His fury burst loose. "What in the *hell* do you think you're doing, Sam?"

The dog looked at him, wagged his tail low and slow, and then open-mouthed a grin at Cora. She approached; her hand out to pet the brat and he accepted her touch on his forehead, a feat that had taken Kal weeks to be allowed to do.

"Oh, for heaven's sake, get in the back and stay there." Sam sniffed in his direction but followed the order. Nimbly, he leapt to his old seat and stuck his nose in the air, a total brushoff if Kal ever saw one.

Cora watched the byplay, laughter filling her voice. "I do believe he's pissed at you for tying him up in the first place. He'd have obeyed the order to stay, wouldn't he?"

"Hell, I don't know. I've never brought him on the road before. We pretty much work in the office, and if I'm off on a case, I leave him at home. So, did you get enough of rattling Nolan's cage back there?"

Cora gunned it and took off up the driveway. They passed the security hut, and Kal thanked God the gates were open. He wasn't too sure of the brakes on the jeep.

With the convertible top, Cora had to raise her voice. "By the time we left, I thought the quack looked a bit green around the gills. I do believe his scheme is starting to unravel. I need to let the officers working in the financial arena know they need to keep a close eye on Mr. Big-Shot II. He could wrap up his game and decide to silently slip away somewhere with no extradition in place. I'd hate to see him escape with the files of where to confiscate what's left of his ill-earned profits. We need to recover as much as possible for his foolish targets."

Kal sensed disgust. "You think they deserve what he's planning to do to them?"

Cora cussed under her breath. "Not really. They're just people trying to make more money from what little they have. He's a smooth talker, has all the answers, and most of his dupes don't stand a chance. What gets in my craw is the bastard doesn't give a flying fuck who he takes along for the ride."

"Please tell me you're not one of the foolish. You seem to have a personal grudge going on here."

"Nah! I'm too cheap to let a swindler get at my pitiful bank account. But he managed to take a load off Sadie before I found out and made her confront him and demand she get her money back."

"Did she?"

"Other than his ridiculous supposed upfront costs, she managed to get most of it returned. But she's like everyone else, out to make a quick buck. I kept telling her, when something seems too good to be true, it's because it is – too bloody good to be true."

Kal laughed, couldn't help himself. Her colorful language would normally have turned him off, but for some reason, her comfort with the words she used to describe how she viewed the world seemed fitting somehow. Before he could ask where they were heading next, a voice came over the car's monitor. "All cars in the vicinity of the Roosevelt Hotel, 130 Roosevelt Way, we have an armed disturbance in the lobby."

Cora clicked in and answered. "Just around the corner. I'll be there in a few minutes. Hang on, Kal. You too, Sam." Swerving the car into an unexpected U-turn, Cora watched the traffic while Kal grabbed for the bar, and Sam skidded forward, catching himself before falling off the seat. He growled even louder than Kal.

"Jesus, Cora. Anyone ever tell you you're a menace behind the wheel?"

"Hey, quit your whining, both of you. We're here quicker because I pulled that stunt. Look."

Chapter
Twenty

Kal couldn't believe it. A man, in front of the hotel doors leading to the gold-plated lobby entrance, stood on top of a wooden box. In his hands, he clutched a high-powered rifle aimed at the crowd who'd stopped to hear his sermon.

"That's right, git on over here and listen to what the Lord has to say. The day of reckoning is near. He's a forgiving God to those whose hearts are pure. But those of you who break his rules every single day need to repent. Now! On your knees."

A few in the group had dropped to the ground and lay there cowering. Others hovered on their knees, their hands in prayer. Cora saw a few inching backward, hoping to hide behind the planters filled with greenery. Only the volley of bullets shot into the air above their heads soon dissuaded them, and they too dropped to the ground.

In fact, as far as the eye could see, the rifleman had garnered the attention he craved. The doorman, plus others, had made it up the stairs leading to the hotel but lingered there unmoving in case he turned in their direction and shot indiscriminately. Which he'd done a number of times already if the cracks and holes in the wall were evidence.

Kal stopped Cora from moving in before any discussion. "What's the plan?"

"I don't have a plan. But he needs to be taken down before he actually hits someone. Got any ideas?"

"Not really. I could try and get his attention while you get in behind him."

"Too late. Sam has already gotten his attention. Look!"

Kal followed her pointing finger to see his crazy dog in front of the religious nutcase. His performance had the crowd relaxing and the so-called minister of God watched in awe too. There sat the ugliest mutt imaginable on his hind legs and his front paws in a prayerlike position.

"Let's go. He's giving us the time we need."

Kal stepped out from behind the car, put his badge inside his shirt so as not to fluster the orator, and walked up to Sam, his voice ringing out. He dragged up every platitude he could remember from memory. "My friends. Even my dog, Sam, knows the truth of this man's words. It is time to repent. God works in mysterious ways. Prayers matter. Hell is waiting for those disbelievers. Right, Reverend?" Kal pointed at the man now transfixed as he watched his crowd being amused by an animal. He lifted the rifle as if to shoot the performer and Kal's heart sped up so fast he thought he'd lose his lunch. He used his body to shield the fur-hound. *When did Sam come to matter so much?*

"That beast is the devil's spawn."

"No. Look! The devil doesn't pray. Look! He's praying, To you. God must have sent him, to you, so he could help you get the folks here to listen to your words."

Kal's heart ramped up when he saw Cora inching up behind the idiot spellbound now with the ideas he'd implanted.

Suddenly, the performer saw a way to use Sam. "Yes! Folks, he's been sent as a sign. All God's creatures need to pray for forgiveness. The world is filled with darkness, he's the light."

"And you're finished." Cora had risen from behind, jabbed the man's knees to topple him over at the same time as she kept control of the rifle so he couldn't raise it and pull the trigger. Once loose, she dropped the weapon behind her and began grappling with the thrasher.

Within seconds, Sam had rushed in and had his jaws around the scrawny neck of the actor, keeping the idiot instantly still, giving Cora the assistance she needed to get on the handcuffs.

In the meantime, Kal had spotted a punk who'd been behind the scenes inch towards the gun. He rushed forward and dove at the fleeing thief, pulling him to the ground while the confiscated rifle lay under them, unusable to anyone.

Kal tried to control the perp, but now the man tussled for his freedom. He'd thought to get away, that no one would see him, never mind tackle him. But Kal had no intention of letting the jerk off with his tricks.

"Let me go. I didn't do anything. I was just controlling the weapon so he couldn't use it again. Let me go, you maniac. I'm a police officer."

Chapter Twenty-one

"Cora, it isn't funny. Tell this guy to let me up."

"It's okay Kal, he's one of us." She bent to take the firearm from under the furious male. "You sure know how to make an appearance, Chuck. I've handcuffed our performer over to the light post, here's the keys. He's your collar, but I want that set back. You wouldn't believe how many of those I've misplaced after paying for the decent cuffs from my own pocket."

Kal stood up and then reached down his hand to help the other man to his feet. "Sorry about this. Didn't know what you were up to, and you weren't wearing a uniform." Now, Kal got a good look at the guy he'd tackled. His brown eyes matched his brown hair and was pretty much in sync with his brown outfit. This guy wouldn't stand out in a crowd and yet could handle himself. Kal just had more training in martial arts and knew how to control a fighter.

"Thanks. Don't worry about it. I should have called out. You seemed a bit preoccupied at the time, and I had the thought to keep the weapon from getting into the wrong hands."

Cora pointed at Kal while speaking to the other man. "Detective Chuck Moray meet Special Agent Hunter from New York. He's working a cold-case with me for now."

Chuck held out his hand, "I made you for FBI from the identification." He pointed to the lanyard with Kal's badge now hanging in plain sight after the struggle. "Pleased to meet you."

Cora handed him the weapon and passed over the bullets she'd emptied also. "You'll need these when you take him in. I called for backup, and they'll be here in a few minutes. Look, Chuck, any one of these fools who've stuck around can tell you what happened. Might want to interview the doorman. I suspect he saw the whole thing. Plus, the video cam they have attached for the entrance will tell the story. We're off to do some real detective work."

Chuck laughed. "Real work, huh? Anytime you're looking for a New Orleans partner, Cora, put me at the top of your list. Never knew another cop where trouble seems to shadow."

Cora grinned. "Quit sweet-talking me." She pointed at the keys in Chuck's pocket and started to move away. "I want those handcuffs back, you hear?"

"How about I give them back over dinner and drinks at Preservation Hall? You like jazz. I've seen you there before."

"How about I give it some thought. Maybe call your girlfriend to join us." She kept walking and was pleased to see Kal nod in Chuck's direction, but follow her, Sam by his side.

Chuck's laughing voice followed, "Don't bother. She left me for a guy with a nine to five job." Chuck's voice came out sounding sad, as he'd obviously intended. "I'll call you."

"You do that."

Cora never looked back, just lifted her fingers to wave. She headed to the parked jeep and reached for the list. Kal, following, would have sworn he saw her moving more suggestively, like a wiggle in her walk. God help him, he had the urge to smack her butt like one would a child and warn her to behave.

Knowing she'd level him, he curbed his instinct, moved to the passenger side, and stopped to pay attention to Sam. The dog sat in front of him with his head stiffly held as if waiting to be reproached for not taking orders.

***

Kal had a lot of frustration to release. From where it took shape, he couldn't say. He only knew that one of the miscreants who'd given him the most angst could now be tackled and wouldn't sass back.

While Sam sat in front of him appearing to not give a hot damn as to what his master had gone through, the reprimand festered. "Sam, do you have any idea what I went through when that jackass pointed his gun at you?"

Sam whined. He lowered his head, looking shamefaced.

"You do that to me again, and I'll find a kennel that'll accept an ugly brute like you and leave you there. You got that?" Kal ground his teeth, a habit he couldn't seem to break since he'd become roommates with the dog. "That'll keep you out of trouble."

As if the dog understood his master's complaints weren't too serious, he nudged against Kal's arm with his snout and then did the most amazing thing. Cora looked as mesmerized as he felt.

Sam had stood on his hind feet, leaned his front paws on Kal's shoulders, and reached up to lather his face with one swoop of his tongue. Kal pushed him away, much gentler than he'd intended. "Stop sucking up." He stroked Sam's head, pointed at the back seat, and muttered, "Get in." From the corner of his eye, he watched Cora trying not to laugh and the words came out of their own accord. "Seriously, lady? Don't encourage him. I'm too old for this shit!"

Chapter
Twenty-two

Cora had never seen anything like it... the bond between Sam and Kal. Dogs and even cats had appeared in different periods of her early years, yet she'd never had an animal herself, nor had a close attachment with one. Not like her friends Sadie or Mona.

While she'd inched her way behind the preacher, Sam had provided the cover she'd needed. Gave her assistance to keep the preacher still so she could use the handcuffs. During the crisis, she'd seen Kal move in front of his pet, using his body to shield the mutt when the rifle had been pointed at him.

That kind of affection threw her for a loop. Made her loosen that particular dam of distaste she'd nurtured of being reliant on an animal or having one dependent on her.

A vision of a tiny white furball rose and stayed

with her. Silly thing had taken a liking to her. Suddenly, a memory formed of her crying into the furry body and clinging to the live creature as she sunk into her particular pit of despair.

The animal had stayed with her, quiet... knowing... licking her face, hands, wherever she could to give the only solace she had in her power.

Was that when the puppy had decided on its new mistress? Jesus, now wasn't the time to think about that nonsense. She turned to Kal who sat next to her, clinging to the front bar, his face pale.

"You okay, Bud?"

"Hell, I'd feel a lot better if you'd let me drive."

He's scared! My driving is making him crazy. Loving the idea, she mentioned the one reason it would be silly for them to change places. "You don't know the city."

"A dead person wouldn't either."

Taking pity, she loosened her foot from the gas pedal. The realization that she'd been speeding and acting more aggressive than usual surfaced and she added, "Sorry. I'll behave. Do you have your weapon on you?"

"Yes. Why?"

"Where we're going to next, you might need it."

"Oh-kay. I'm wearing an ankle holster I use when I'm off duty or don't expect to need a gun."

"Good. I'm not saying there'll be trouble, but we're walking into a den of rattlers, and they're venomous. Best to be aware, have protection, and stay close. Wouldn't mind having Sam with us this time. He'll be added protection. Many of these street people have guard dogs, so he'll help keep the peace."

"Where are we going?"

"We're here." Cora pulled to the curb, went to the back of the jeep, and lifted out a couple of Kevlar vests, handing the larger one to Kal. "There's a taser in the pocket." She looked down at Sam who'd followed Kal's hand signal to join them. "I'm sorry I don't have one for you, Sam. They make them for the dogs, but I never knew we'd have Sam with us. We'll have to go to where they issue equipment at the department and get one for him."

"Not sure he'll be with us again. Today was a one-off."

"Too bad. He's been a good pal to have along. But it's your call."

"So, is there a specific person you're going to seek out here?"

"There're a couple. One sells drugs and keeps close contact with his various distributors who do a lot of business around here. And the other is a known pedophile who doesn't get hassled by those who care more about their next hit than the people living in their neighboring tent."

"Please tell me there aren't any children caught up in this slum."

"Not that I'm aware of. As soon as one arrives,

we have a system where either myself or my department is notified by a caring individual, and we send the social workers in to extract them. This sure as shit isn't a place for kids."

Cora started forward into the shaded alley, feeling protected by Kal and Sam. Funny how some people did that for you, made you aware that they'd do anything in their power to keep you safe.

Things hadn't changed since the last time she'd visited a month ago. Some new structures, a lot more garbage, a blended urine and garbage stench that couldn't be accurately described, and wretched folks turning away or inching inside their temporary dwellings.

Following the twisting path, she saw the overwhelming poverty, rusted store buggies filled to the brim with pure junk that a person would die to protect, tent-like plastic structures rigged more for shade and privacy rather than a sense of a home, and bodies helter-skelter, lying against walls often with only a bit of cardboard to separate them from the dirt.

Life here never changed. Just the people. Deaths from overdoses, bad drugs, and rotten health might bring the numbers down if it hadn't been for the newly hooked moving in.

Kal whispered, "Which way? Sam's getting nervous."

Cora could see that Sam stuck close, growled at any barkers, and showed his teeth to those yapping dogs with an attitude. Maybe his size made the difference, or could be his demeanor, but he wasn't rushed, and neither were his people hassled.

Until they approached a corrugated roof structure hanging from the back of a building. Cora stopped and called out, "Hank, I know you're there. Ammo's out here acting up. Look, I just want to talk with you. Call off your dog and be hospitable."

Ammo, the huge German Shephard mix, didn't like people, and he sure as hell didn't like other dogs who were bigger and scarier than himself. One could see him sizing up Sam. He pranced back and forth, his vicious noise making Cora nervous.

She took out her taser and aimed it at the festering dog and watched as he instantly backed off and laid down, ears back, teeth gleaming, watchful, complaining, but knowing the power of the instrument she held. It wasn't the first time he'd seen it or felt the taste of it. She'd used it once before and just snagged his tail, but that had been enough for the dog to remember and have respect for her and the people with her.

The plastic door covering pushed aside and a fat man appeared in the opening, a Grizzly Adams beard covering up many of the sores on his face. Beady eyes peered through gray eyebrows hanging every which way and a huge belly protruded over the sagging jeans waistband that cried for a belt. "Long time, Ma'am." He hitched up his pants for them to slide down again within seconds. "Now you're back." He cleaned the hole between his front teeth with a dirty fingernail, emanating a disgusting sucking sound. "Too bad."

"You ever form a whole sentence, Hank?" Cora slipped her taser back in her pocket, not wanting to rile up the big guy.

"Nope. Whose dog?"

"Mine." Kal crossed his arms and kept his face blank, not letting the shock appear.

"Good looker."

"You blind?"

"What's up?" Hank looked at them and then turned to Ammo, making a motion that the dog understood.

Cora had seen that command before and could do nothing to stop it once given. Son of a bitch! That bastard Hank got a kick out of dogs fighting and was always on the lookout for a fiercer dog than Ammo.

Once given the sign, Ammo savagely attacked, rushing Sam. The big dog seemed to expect this treatment and had turned, protecting his neck, and then twisting away so he could go for Ammo's scruff in a counterattack.

The growls deafened and made Cora's stomach twist, her nerves rotating like crazy. Goddamn, she'd known the dogs were vicious around this place. Hadn't she been bitten already before getting wise and carrying a taser? But the two fighters moved so fast, it was impossible to aim with any surety of hitting the right target.

Before Cora could do anything, Kal had his gun out, had grabbed the vicious animal off Sam from behind in a choke hold and aimed the weapon at Ammo's head. Sam stayed close, his dripping fangs inches from Ammo's muzzle. "Either call off your dog, Hank, or I'll pull the trigger. This isn't a game."

"Ammo. Down." Instantly the fight left the Shephard. He wriggled from Kal's hold, ignored the warning from a still furious Sam, and moved closer to Hank.

"You selling?" Hank pointed at Sam.

"You for real?"

"I have money."

"Which you can stick up your ass."

Hank turned back to Cora who'd stood ready to step in if she'd have been needed. "What?"

"I'm here to warn you. There's a killer on the loose who seems to be attracted to lawbreakers like yourself, crooks the law hasn't caught up with." She smiled without any humor. "Yet."

"You warning me?"

"That's about it. I know you're a small-time kingpin for most of the drugs available around this district. And I know you provide a lot of sellers with their product. Yet, I also know you're particular about the grade of drugs you sell, that people trust you, and you've won that trust. Kinda figure you're the best of the worst. So, yeah, I'm warning you. Get a few bodyguards to keep an eye open for a while. This guy means business, and he seems to have a way of getting through to the people who feel the most protected."

"Who is he?"

"We don't know. He started a killing spree ten years ago. We never caught him then, and he stopped before we could. A short while ago, he started up again, same MO, same random choices, only this time, he's going after those the law hasn't arrested yet. People like you."

"Like me? He kill Hank?"

"If you let him. Call me if anything happens. We need him off the streets."

The big man had nothing more to say and with a nod at Cora, and a piercing glare at Kal followed by a regretful glance Sam's way, he turned back inside the tent-like structure. A grunt sounded that made Ammo follow reluctantly.

Cora looked at Kal who was paying attention to the torn skin on Sam's neck. The blood looked congealed, and the dog seemed annoyed at the attention, backing away.

Feeling a visceral reaction like when one sees something painful and the body instinctively sensitizes, her response hit her hard and had to be shaken off. "Is he okay?" She moved to Sam and reached out her hand.

The dog let her close in and even pat his back

before moving away as if to say, "Quit fussing. I'm fine."

Kal looked at her and said exactly what she was thinking. "I guess he's alright. Who else do we need to contact before we can leave this depressing hole?"

***

Kal couldn't believe he'd meddled in a dog fight. If anyone had told him he'd be doing something that idiotic, he'd have laughed and told them to get a shrink. Thankfully, there'd been no time to ponder his choices, he'd just reacted.

Grabbing his gun, he'd watched for the instant when he could interfere and did so. The snarling animals had moved with such speed, he still had to shake his head at the fact he'd gotten that second of opportunity.

Would Sam have won? He couldn't be sure. It looked like he had the grit, but his mangy opponent had scars to prove his fighting prowess.

If Hank hadn't called him off, would he have shot Ammo?

In a heartbeat...

And the thought made him sorry as hell. Desperation drove a man, and he'd been on the brink. Now if that mangy mutt had attacked Cora, he wouldn't have hesitated long enough to make any demands at Hank.

That absolute truth shook the shit out of him. When did she start mattering more than Sam?

And when did the dog sneak into his heart?

Chapter Twenty-thre e

Kal kept his hand on Sam's collar as they continued further into the alley. The dog didn't like being held this way and glared at Kal. "Too bad, buddy. You stay with me. No more getting into trouble."

Cora led the way and approached a woman who pretended she saw nothing. Stopping to speak, Cora glanced all around but there was no doubt who her words were meant for. "You okay, May? How's the cold?"

"I'm fine. Took some drugs for that fucker, and it cleared up." She laughed as if she'd made a joke, and Kal saw that Cora smiled along, as if she got the humor too. Not part of their inside joke, he didn't say anything, just stood behind the female cop, watching her back.

"Any news you need to share?"

"Not lately. It's quiet around here for a change."

"You got my number. Use it if you see anything strange, you hear?"

"Yeah. This mean you're expecting trouble?"

"Not sure. There's a man on the loose. Likes to kill people randomly and his victims all have one thing in common. They're folks the law hasn't caught up with yet. So be careful and keep your eyes open for strangers. I'd be grateful to hear from you if you learn anything about this bastard."

"Understood." May wrapped her dirty, faded, flowered mumu around her scrawny body and walked toward a lopsided umbrella, a huge, faded thing that had seen better days but could still provide some sanction from the sun or rain.

Cora stepped into his space so she could talk low. "That's May, probably the person who's been here the longest. She's good people no matter which personality she's using, and I've encountered three so far."

Kal's amazement showed before he could hide it from her. "She's schizophrenic? Looks to me like an ordinary old lady down on her luck who doesn't belong here. She have any particular addiction?"

"If you mean does she do drugs or alcohol? No, that's not her problem. She's lost in her head a lot of the time and around here, people don't care. They leave her alone, and she gets to live her way without hassles. Her choice. I offered to take her to the home where my mom lives, and she hid from me for almost a year before I could make her understand it was only a suggestion. I'd never use force. She's just begun to trust me again."

"And she keeps you updated about what's happening in this weird community."

"For a small monthly fee. I leave a couple of twenties in a Post Office box and she helps keep the peace. A perfect arrangement. It's not a big deal. Works both ways."

Kal caught Cora's eye when he saw her blush. Who did that anymore?

He'd bet his paycheck she left more than a few twenties each month. She's shy about caring for someone in need. His heart brightened. He liked that about her. Liked that a poor old woman mattered.

Over the years, he'd tried to be a thoughtful son to his mom, make her as happy as he could, and be a good citizen. In his own way, he worked in the community at various times, volunteering at the food bank during celebration days when they needed the extra hands on board.

The police in the district of New York were often occupied with charitable campaigns, and he'd helped organize his share. He just never imagined he'd be so entranced by another cop who had the same sense of humanity and still be able to blush about it. Instinctively, he stepped closer to her and wished she had a collar he could hold on to, like Sam.

A man came into view and she nodded toward him. "There's Tom. He's the pedophile I told you about. But there's more to the story."

"Okay. Tell me." Kal saw an older black man, still good-looking in today's modern society. He wore a lot of tattoos, all over his arms and hands, but the ones on his bald head and cheek distracted and caught the eye. He looked sober until one saw his eyes and correctly gathered he had more than a few drinks in him. "I sense there's a story here."

Cora stopped and began sharing. "He was a top executive with a huge law firm, made a lot of money and owned a big house. He never hooked up seriously, not until he got involved with a white woman, and for the first time, he wanted to get married. It wasn't until the week before the wedding that she admitted she had a family of three girls ranging from nine to thirteen who'd been looked after by her mother. That lady suddenly became ill and couldn't be the caretaker for her kids anymore. It meant she had to take over custody herself."

"She'd kept it from him, her own kids?"

"Yep. That was the plan all along. He was so infatuated, he agreed to still marry her. Said they could have the kids live with them."

"So, what happened?"

"Within a few months, the oldest daughter claimed he'd come into her bedroom and raped her. They called 911. I was the attending officer. The scene blew my mind. The daughter remained in a trance-like state after she'd made her mind-blowing accusations. He'd had a few drinks earlier, nothing abnormal. The mother had gone visiting a girlfriend and left him home with the kids. The daughter waited for the mom's return and accused him of coming to her room and assaulting her. His story totally contradicted that. He'd heard a noise and when he'd gone to investigate, her window had been open, a figure could be seen running from the property and, she was totally disheveled and out of control."

"She'd been attacked?"

"According to her, he'd been her attacker. There had been signs of sexual activity once we took her to the hospital, but no DNA to prove who the culprit had been. Obviously, the abuser had worn a condom."

"So, he took the fall."

"Not quite that simple. The mother believed her daughter right from the beginning, and he was charged. But he had such a good reputation, it would have been a 'he said, she said' situation for the jury to decide. Until the sister stepped up."

"The youngest?"

"Yeah, the nine-year-old. And she did so in such a way as to sway the outcome. She waited until his lawyer had begun their closing argument. Shocking everyone, she stood up in the courtroom and accused him of coming on to her too. That pretty well ended his chances. He served eight years and got out a year ago on good behavior."

"What happened to his wife?"

"She lived off his money as long as it held up, and then talked him into giving her the right to sell his house."

"That's terrible." Kal sensed there was more. "You believed him."

"Yep. You had to have been there that night. The girl could win an academy award for her performance, but the mom could take the Golden Globe. I smelled a setup right from the beginning."

"Did you get the chance to say that in court?"

"I tried but the prosecutor held me to yes and no answers, giving me no leeway, and his questions were compiled in such a way as to be damning to the defense. When Tom had his chance to let me share my opinion, the prosecutor interrupted so often, contradicting me, my words were more of a hindrance. You see, I had no solid evidence, just my gut instincts."

"They convicted him."

"In the end, he took a plea, spent those years in jail, and from the day he got out, he's been here, him and his bottle."

"You believe he's innocent?"

"Hell, I don't know. Many believe he got a sweet bargain. Me... I believe he believes he's innocent. Does that count?"

"Sorry. That's too deep for me. Now, you're warning him because...?"

"He deserves to stay alive. I keep my fingers crossed that one day he might sober up long enough to give a shit about what's left of his future. The girls are older now. Maybe they've grown a conscience. I know his wife didn't end up well. Five years ago, she took her own life. Often wondered if the guilt finally caught up with her."

"Jesus, that's a sad tale. Okay, let's warn him and call it a day. This place gives me the willies, and I'd prefer not to be here once the sun goes down."

"Seriously?"

"Seriously. Listen, it's quiet now and who knows for how long. We both need to eat. Plus, I love jazz. If you're a good girl, I'll take you to that Preservation Hall tonight for a meal." He winked to let her know he was teasing.

Her finger went up toward his face, and her eyes glowed with humor. "You talking to Sam or me?" She sneered. "If I'm a good girl... You're nuts." Chuckling her delight at their sparring, she replied, "Hmm, I do like to eat there, and I can suffer a night of good jazz anytime... no matter who I'm with. Right, give me a few minutes to talk to Tom, let him know he needs to be careful, and you have a deal." She added before moving, "Your idea, you pay."

"Me? I have to pay?" He stared at her straight face. "Fine."

Cora continued walking, giggling as he intended. "So, the big New York Agent is a scaredy-cat deep down."

"Hey, who said I was scared?"

"You said the place gave you the willies."

"Me and my big mouth."

Chapter Twenty-four

Cora got a kick out of Kal's tactics. She saw through his ploy of wanting to get her away from the hideous place and protect her. Mind you, he was right about the wretched alley giving her the heebie-jeebies too. She only went in there when it was totally necessary. Funny thing, every time she did so, she appreciated her own life a hell of a lot more.

They left after Tom ignored her warning, using words such as, "I hope it's me he chooses to kill. He'd be doing me a favor."

"Tom, you need to snap out of this self-indulgent bullshit pit you're in here and find a way to prove your innocence. I'll help any way I can, but it's on you, bud."

"Why, Cora. Why bother? It's been too long. Besides, they believed her story, not mine. It's the same old race thing."

"Hey, don't go there. You never fought. As soon as little Nora lied about her involvement, you buckled."

Tom shot her a look of anger. "Because I had no choice. I did try to make friends with the girl. One night, she was scared, crying. I went into her room to console her. Christ, Cora, she was only nine years old and she was frightened of the storm. I picked her up in my arms, carried her to the chair, and rocked her for a long time. I felt so sorry for the kid, so damn sorry for her uncontrollable fear. She might have been nine, but she reacted to the noise like a baby. I kissed her hair and held her, thinking what a great dad I made. And she turned that special moment into a disgusting event."

"And you let her."

"I was hurt. Don't you understand what it does to a man when his best intentions are dragged through the mud? That girl lied to save her sister, maybe she even believed I'd done wrong, I don't know. They hadn't had a man in their lives for years before me. And I had no prior experience with kids. I didn't know how to get through to her." Frustration lit his eyes to hardened black shards of coal. "Give it up, Cora. Let it go and leave me the hell alone." Tom turned his back, lifted his bottle, and drained the last quarter in one gulp.

She left. And the sadness followed. Damn, she'd give anything to get through to him. But the wall he'd erected wouldn't be breached.

His choice.

Her failure.

They headed back to their vehicle, and she called in to the office to see if there had been anything new on their case.

Suddenly, she felt a lick on her hand and instinctively knew Sam had sensed her turmoil and tried to make her feel better. It did.

Looking around, she saw the reason Sam had been free. Kal had his phone to his ear and his distraction to their surroundings let her know something was up.

She began walking to the exit, and both males followed her. Once the call had been disconnected, she asked, "What's wrong?"

"Freddie found a few more addresses from your list and says he's concerned about one of the names."

"Which one?"

"Former Governor, Patrick Holmes. Seems he got away with defrauding the government a few years back and though they tried to press charges, they never stuck. He's a bad apple, had a few domestic disturbance calls and his wife refused to press charges. He's kind of a smutty character. You know anything about him?"

"Yeah, he's a mover and shaker. Never knew an individual who could turn on so much charm whenever he had his back against the wall. Had the people here eating out of his hands for years. Many still believe he got railroaded, and he should be in office."

"What's your opinion?"

"Me? I think the jerk should be behind federal bars serving a major sentence for bribery, fraud, extortion and money-laundering."

"Yet you didn't convict him?" Kal urged Sam into the back seat. Though he looked at the rope, he didn't bother.

"Not my job. Those who checked into the matter couldn't get enough evidence to make the charges stick."

"I thought in those cases they followed the money trail."

"He'd paid off too many higher-ups, so the trail never led them to any supporting evidence. Man could afford the best lawyers. Who knows, he probably had the previous prosecuting attorney in his pocket too. The corruption in this city was rampant."

Kal leaned on the jeep and stroked Sam's nearby head. "You said... was."

"Things began to improve a few years ago. They elected a new Governor and Police Superintendent. I believe those men were instrumental in turning things around and forcing changes for the better. Not surprisingly, a few of the top officials decided to retire from public office around that time. Others, like Holmes, were charged, but no convictions. It's better now, but we still need to be vigilant. Those types of criminals are smart, and they crave the power of the office."

"He's put his name in the race again."

"Yep. How did you know?"

"It's one of the reasons Freddie was concerned. You know where we can find this man?"

"Usually, they hold government functions in the capital, Baton Rouge, but I read there's a gala function tonight on the Creole Queen here in New Orleans."

"Creole Queen? Sounds like a ship."

"It's a restored paddle-wheeler we have here for the tourists, but it can also be rented for special occasions. It's huge and a favorite amongst the bigshots. Guess Holmes will be attending tonight. Why is that a worry? What's Freddie's other reason for being concerned?"

"Looks like there was a murder in New Orleans ten years ago which was a drowning. It happened on this date and was exactly seven days before the next murder. The same schedule as our guy."

"True. It happened at the same location the Creole Queen travels, too. But that we never made it for the cold-case killer. There was no evidence left at the scene. Christ, the body was found floating in the river."

"Uh huh. But he'd been drowned. And the weapon there could have been the river itself. Who's to say he hadn't done it? And Freddie's concerned he might be focusing on the Mayor and planning to make a move tonight."

"So much for our plans. Looks like we'll be crashing a closed event instead. Do you have a tux packed in your gear?" Cora shook her head. She'd have to pull out her much-worn little black dress one more time.

Chapter Twenty-five

Kal knew it was a party city, but even he was shocked at the ease he had of renting a tuxedo late on a Friday afternoon. His usual revulsion in wearing the same outfit other men had worn had to be overcome, and it took a lot of discussion, mainly him berating himself, to stop being such a picky prick.

Sometimes things had to be done for the sake of the job, yada, yada. And the job came first, blah, blah. The fact that Cora needed an escort had been pushed to the back of his mind, and yet if he were honest, it was the principal reason he swallowed his fears and accepted there was no choice. He'd promised to pick her up in a few hours, and by golly, he'd be there and dressed in his monkey suit looking like a typical groom at a swanky wedding.

To keep his mind active, he worked the files from his laptop and waited for Freddie to arrive so he could leave Sam with him. A boat would be no place for his mutt companion tonight and the thought made him even more anxious.

Once he'd settled everything at the hotel, he took a cab to Cora's house and found her wearing a gorgeous black dress that fit her snugly to the waist and flared out from the hips in a filmy kind of see-through skirt that moved with every step. The swathe of material that covered her chest was held there only by tiny rhinestone straps. Ones he feared might snap if she moved too fast.

His eyes fixated on the amount of skin open for any man's eyes, and the soft mounds of breast available for attention. Unable to turn away, words broke free he never intended to say. "You should wear a sweater."

"It's ninety-five degrees outside."

"Right. Maybe just a scarf to cover up your... ahh, front."

Cora laughed as if he'd told a huge joke. "You're funny."

"Am I? I wasn't trying to be." Kal had to grin as if he were fibbing once again. To cover up his blunder, he added truthfully, "You look lovely."

"Thanks." She reached for her black high-heeled sandals with rhinestones on the straps and wrapped them around her feet and up her ankles. While doing so, she added, "Some men can wear a tux much better than others."

He didn't want to ask her which category he fit

into, and he could see she got a kick out of the teasing way she'd worded her statement. Rather than agreeing or saying thanks, he outwaited the silence, and she finally grinned. "I traded for Mona's car for tonight so we could arrive in style and not all disheveled."

"Good idea. Does she live close?"

"Further up the street about two blocks. She's good people."

"Seems like. How's she doing with the pups?"

"Other than being pissed at me for leaving her to deal with the wailer, I think they've settled okay. Charli, the mother dog is a good girl and takes care of her babies."

"And the wailer, I suppose, is the one who took to you earlier. The one who fought to stay with you. Damnedest thing I ever saw. It was like she'd decided you needed her."

"Yeah, took me some time to settle her again before Mona would let me leave. We had to trick her so she could take her into the other room, poor, sweet baby."

"Holy hell, if you used that tone and those words with her, no wonder she didn't want you to leave."

Cora knew Kal was teasing but it wasn't funny when she saw the little fluffball actually crying, tears filling her eyes as if heartbroken when she went to pass her back over to Mona.

Why the hell she went there knowing she'd see the pups beat her. She knew better. But something inside her had to see if she'd imagined the reaction from the little fluff-muffin, the total adoration she'd sensed. Turns out, the mutt had fallen for her, and now Cora had the feeling that it might be reciprocated. *God help her, a puppy? Seriously?*

In a short time, they arrived at the Creole Queen's berth, and using the fake invitations Freddie concocted, they proceeded up the gangplank to converge with many other partygoers on deck.

It seems they made it just in time before the ship left the dock and traveled on the usual course along the river, the gentle breezes transforming the warmth of the night to a bearable level.

It had been some time since Cora had been on the paddle-wheeler, and she certainly didn't remember it decked out with the amount of bling shown tonight. There were bouquets of flowers set up in urns, decorating many of the corners with twinkle lights added that brought them to life.

The music piped everywhere gave a real party atmosphere as did the lit-up bar arrangement in the far corner sporting various bottles of champagne, sparkling glasses ranging in different sizes, and arrangements of cocaine lines on mirrored platters waiting for the sniffers who preferred this kind of lift. On the wall behind the bar, they displayed most every brand of expensive liquor available.

Seems like the Former Governor, Patrick

Holmes, wanted to win a lot of the rich and famous over to his side again and was using this ridiculous flouting of wealth to do so.

When a waiter balancing a tray of filled champagne flutes walked past and offered drinks, Cora helped herself, as did Kal. They took their time while sipping the cool beverage to scrutinize the surroundings and see if they could spot the man of the hour.

Kal caught her attention with his curiosity. "Tell me again why we couldn't have just gone to the man's home or office to pass on the warning?"

"Because we think there might be a murder here tonight, and if we catch the killer in the act, we'd end this farce once and for all."

"Right. I knew there was more to it than just you wanting to show off that outfit."

Cora chuckled. "What is it about this dress that offends you. From the first moment you saw me, you've worn a slightly sour expression and you seem out of sorts."

"Nah! You've got me all wrong. I love the dress. Just think it might look better teamed with a t-shirt and maybe a slip." He sipped his drink and refused to meet her gaze.

"You know, I *think* you're teasing. But I'm not sure... ahh, since we're crashing the party tonight wasn't it the plan that we wouldn't stand out. Don't I look like every other woman here tonight?"

Kal's head swiveled to face her, his expression

astonished. "Not by a long shot. You're stunning. They're ordinary. We weren't supposed to bring attention to ourselves, right? Here you are with your hair all puffed up like it took six hours at the hairdresser's to get that style. On top of that, you're made up like some famous model with all that makeup... nope, you sure didn't try to keep things low key."

"Well asshole, you have no room to talk. That tux sure as shit doesn't make you look like most of the other fatties in the room either. So there." Cora didn't know whether she'd just been complimented or dissed. She snuck a peek at Kal's sour expression to see him wearing a huge smile instead.

Ha! He liked her noticing how he looked. It mattered to him. Bastard! It bloody-well didn't matter to her that he thought she was stunning. Yet the one thing Freddie had told her as they'd worked together earlier for a few moments on the invitations was the reason it thrilled him to be teamed with Kal had to do with the man's honor. He had it in spades. If Kal gave his word, it was gospel. He never lied or bullshitted, and one could rely on that knowledge.

Cora felt a warmth begin to blossom inside her. No matter how she wanted them gone, she couldn't stop the exciting sensations from taking hold. It seems that Special Agent Hunter might have the hots for her.

Cool!

"Well, well, good evening, Detective. And why, may I ask, do we have the pleasure of your uninvited company tonight?"

"Good evening, Governor. Nice shindig. Any chance you can get the fellows to change the tapes? That god-awful elevator music sure can get on one's nerves."

The governor laughed and turned to Kal. "I don't believe I've had the pleasure, sir?"

"Nope, don't suppose you have. I'm Special Agent Kal Hunter on assignment from New York. It's the reason we decided to appear tonight in person. We're here to warn you."

Patrick Holmes genially offered his hand. "I don't understand. What would I have to do with an assignment you're on from New York?"

"It's a long story, Sir. One you might or might not be personally involved with. You see we're expecting a drowning to happen sometime tonight, and we think you might be the victim."

"Me? I'm surrounded by a hundred or more people, and I plan to keep going till the early hours. How in the world would this maniac get to me? I think you must be mistaken and have the wrong man." Patrick's perplexed look changed to one of worry. He looked around at everyone and then turned back to Cora. "This social event is by invitation only. No one would be onboard who wasn't supposed to be here."

"And yet here we are. And we weren't invited." Cora grinned, hoping the evil in her mind didn't show on her face. This pompous prick thought himself inaccessible because of his stature.

"Look, Mr. Holmes, our killer went on a spree ten years ago, faded from sight, and has recently returned to do more killing, using the same MO as before. Only this time, he's specific and only kills those people who have cheated the system and gotten away with it, especially if those broken laws hurt others. Like insider trading and money laundering."

Patrick Holmes bristled, expressing anger. "If you're accusing me of these crimes, you have the wrong guy."

Cora had to add, "No. We just didn't make our case in court against you because of technicalities your fancy lawyers came up with. But you're guilty as sin, Holmes, and the killer seems to know these things. We believe tonight his victim will suffer from drowning. Just watch your back. And call us if you see any red flags."

Holmes sneered at her assumptions and bowed slightly. "Have a lovely evening, my dear. Sir." Before he turned away, he added nonchalantly, "Tomorrow I'll make sure they pull both your badges, so you might as well make the most of tonight." This time he stomped over to the bar, and Cora watched him give instructions to the bodyguard hovering close.

"I think we rattled his cage just now, don't you?"

"Enough that he figures he has enough connections to get us both fired."

"Are you worried?"

"Worried? Why? Aren't we here to stop the numbskull from getting killed? Isn't that what we do... Serve and Protect. Hell, no. I'd say we're just doing our jobs, going above and beyond the call of duty. Dance?"

Cora laughed. She loved his way of looking at the situation, and she could tell he meant every word. The man had a way of getting under her armor. She moved into his waiting arms and was lost. Just like that. God Almighty, he smelled wonderful, his cologne pure magic. His arms were gentle and his hand warm... oh so... so warm.

Her face against his cheek started sparks, and she pulled back to look into his eyes. She had to see if the magic was happening only to her. His dark gaze had lost all humor. Only passion flared as he breathed deeply, pulled her in closer, and groaned.

Chapter Twenty-six

What the hell just happened? Kal had grown to be very aware of Cora, yes, but as a fellow cop. Not as a woman. Not as the stunning creature he now held in his arms.

Her body was pliant and supple, moving in to his, her chin resting against his shoulder and her soft hair brushing his cheek. Noticing her tiny waist, he scooped her closer. He glanced sideways and the lights made her rhinestone earrings blind him for seconds as they jangled to her bare shoulder.

The same shoulder he wanted to kiss so badly, it felt like a raw ache in his chest. His hand tightened on hers, and he noticed hers clinging harder. Was she as affected as Kal? He had to know.

He leaned back slightly to see those blue shockers staring into his, the deep velvety gaze drawing at him so he could sink in the softness of her questioning stare. He lowered his head. They were just inches apart, breath to breath, nose to nose, and then as if it were meant to happen... lips to lips.

Without planning it, he'd maneuvered them to an alcove of the deck where they were virtually alone by the railing. He gathered her completely into his arms and tasted the woman as thoroughly as he'd ever done before. He wanted to swallow her whole. God, this felt so right... so wonderful.

Her arms had risen around his neck, her chest plastered to his and his hands held her as close as possible without her moving through cloth and skin to meld with him in spirit.

Man, oh man, her lips tasted as wonderful as they looked. He couldn't get enough of her mouth, her neck, even the softness of her shoulders. When his lips traveled to her chest, she stood on tiptoe to make his wandering easier. Neither of them heard the splash, not until the screams followed.

By the time Kal had come back to earth to realize there was a problem, Cora was already removing her shoes, climbing the railing, and balancing on the opposite side. "No!" He made a grab to stop her only to feel her arm yank from his hand before she hit the water.

Son of a bitch...

He hated cold water.

He hated *dark* cold water even more. He removed his own shoes all the while cussing his disgust. When the waiter close enough to hear the distraction appeared, he yelled instructions of "man overboard, get help" and within seconds, he too dove into the dark depths.

The shock of the icy cold wetness brought him out of the love-fog he'd been enjoying seconds earlier. He began swimming to where he saw thrashing and splashes. "Cora? Answer me?"

In no time, he'd reached the area in the darkness where his new partner fought to hang on to a man who'd stopped moving. Terrified to lose the victim, she'd tried to maneuver the body so she could keep his head out of the water, only to be suddenly pulled under by some force wanting to keep her away from the drowning man. As her body disappeared, her clinging hands had flipped the male over before she let go.

What the fuck? What the hell was happening? Kal noticed the body now face down and reversed it hoping against hope that with him no longer swallowing water, though unconscious, he might still be alive and would float.

In the meantime, Kal had also grabbed for Cora, trying to keep her from disappearing, but another force pulling her under had different plans. The murderer had to be hidden in those waves. One who'd wanted her to let go of the man he'd just gone to the trouble of killing.

Frantic to find her, Kal dove repeatedly but could see nothing in the black swirls. His heart triple-timed and his brain refused to accept she might have been swallowed by the depths.

No breath left, forced to rise to the surface, he was just in time to see movement about ten feet away. White limbs were being forced above the water as if someone from below was holding the head up to get air.

Jesus, was the killer now saving her? Kal made multiple promises to God and every deity he knew the whole time it took to reach her. When he arrived to find her weak but alive, he whipped her into his arms thinking to never, ever let the blasted woman leave them.

Sputtering, forcing her toward where a lifesaving team had formed with a small boat having been lowered from the Creole Queen, he muttered blasphemies and threats the whole way. "I can't take my eyes off you for one second, can I? What's with this crazy Super Cora stuff? Thinking you can save the world. You should have been spanked more as a kid." Then he kissed her still face over and over as he swam their bodies forward where they'd be picked up.

When the males in the boat reached for her body, which was slowly gaining consciousness, Kal left them to haul her in and went back to where he knew the other body should have been. Except it had disappeared.

Had the underwater menace finished the job so that the body now lay at the bottom of the river?

Kal had no idea. He only knew that they were too late. The man was dead.

And thank God, Cora was alive.

Chapter Twenty-seve n

Cora hadn't had time to think, she just responded. Someone needed help and she was a paid helper... as simple as that. But hitting that cold water had also reacted on her, had woken her to the harsh reality of the preciousness of life.

Never having spent a great deal of time in a pool as a youngster, she knew how to swim, but couldn't say it was one of her best skills, not like her shooting or driving abilities. Mostly swimming to her was just staying alive in the water. And here she was trying to keep another person alive too.

From the time she reached the body, life became a crazy mix of struggling to breathe, trying to keep another person from drowning, and having to fight off an attacker. The very one who, at that moment, was pulling her under to get her away from his prey, then guiding her to the surface so she wouldn't be a victim also.

It had to be one of the most surreal times she'd ever experienced. Should she be thankful for being saved? Of course, she was. Fervently thankful. Ridiculously over the moon thankful. Wanting to jump for joy with thankfulness.

Did it shock her that Kal had come to her rescue? Big time. Christ Almighty, that man was getting to her. She needed to rethink her reactions to him.

Later...

Was she pissed that the same killer who took the governor's life saved hers? How could she be? Once she found out the name of the dead man, she accepted that shit happens, and sometimes one just has to let go.

"How can you be so calm?" Kal hadn't left her side the whole time they had her in the infirmary on board the boat. When they docked, he made sure an ambulance waited to collect her and take her to the hospital. All that fuss she accepted, but if he didn't let up soon with the nagging, she'd be begging for a gun.

"Would you stop beating on me? I'm fine. I'm as fine as I was the last ten times I told you so."

"You were drowned. Or close enough. I can't believe you can just accept it as if stuff like that happens to you all the time."

Cora hid her grin. If he knew how often she'd been close to death in the last ten years, he'd really lose his cookies. "Hunter, stop. Breathe. Look, I agreed to come to the hospital because you insisted, didn't I? I'm being a good girl like you begged. So, can we drop this whole conversation and get to one that I need to know about?"

Kal looked pouty, but he did agree. "Okay, what?"

"You say that the governor was there onboard when the lifeboat returned to the ship, right? Then who was missing?"

"They weren't sure, hadn't had enough time to check the invitation list against those at the party. We'll know soon enough. Freddie and the team were on their way to set up a search and to deal with the rest of the partygoers. But you're right about one thing. It wasn't the governor the maniac was after."

"Not surprising, I guess. He hung around with a lot of rich assholes who played the system as if it were their right. Many of those powermongers believe they can get away with anything. I wouldn't be surprised if any number of those characters fit in the same thieving mold as Patrick Holmes. It was just that he had the most exposure."

The door opened and the doctor arrived, test results on his tablet and a grin on his face. "And here you are again, Superwoman. I've missed you lately."

Cora played along as usual. "I felt your anxiety, Doc McDreamy. Came to relieve you of your worries. See, I'm fine." She stood, waved her arms in the air, and twirled.

Annoyed that Kal shot up to reach for her, she slapped his hands away and growled, "Sign that blasted form already and let me outta here. You know this place gives me the willies."

Laughing, the older doctor nodded. "You're good to go. I think you might have swallowed some water, but your lungs look fine now. Just take things easy for a few days. No stress, no—"

"Yeah, yeah. I know. Don't move or breathe too deeply. I've heard that so often, it's embedded in my memory."

"Listen here, Mini Mouse, you behave, or I'll call your mama, and then you'll get the what-for."

Pretending shock and fear, Cora stood as a damsel in distress with her hands against her heart. "No, anything else but that, McDreamy. I'll do *anythinggg*."

Obviously enjoying her performance, the doc gave her a quick hug and added, "Behave missy. I mean it. As much as I love your pretty face, I hope to see it anywhere but here. Now scat."

***

Kal loved watching the byplay of the two in front of him and had a hard time not cheering when the doctor gave her instructions to behave. Her reaction should have shocked him but didn't, he just had to stop the chuckles from bursting out. *What a little minx!*

Problem was that little minx had become the most important person in his world. How the hell could he deal with this? She lived life her way... off the cuff and bat-shit crazy. He needed organization and limits. How could that work? Pushing aside his worries, he followed her from the hospital, watching her in the scrubs the nurse had lent her to replace her destroyed gown.

Devoid of makeup and her blonde hair fluffed around her face in all directions, one could have mistaken her for a teenager. Even her swagger appeared wrong somehow until one looked into her cool, knowing eyes.

Totally focused on her job, she said, "First stop to the house to change and then the office to find out where the hell we went wrong."

Chapter Twenty-eigh t

"You're serious? I thought you were kidding when you said you'd change and then go into work. You do know you almost drowned tonight?"

Cora looked at the taxi driver watching them in the rearview mirror and arched her head. "Eyes forward, Mickey."

"Yes, Ma'am. Just haven't seen you wearing a nurse's outfit for a while now. Everything okay, Cora? There's a doc with you."

"Nah, he's no doctor. Just a cop in borrowed clothes. Can you take me home and then drop my partner off at his hotel?"

"Partner? You?"

"He's from New York. We borrowed him for a short time. Drive."

"Yes, Ma'am."

"You're serious?"

Cora had heard the worry in Kal's tone, or she would have leveled him for trying to interfere with her decisions. Instead, patiently, she spoke sweetly, "Yes."

"Yes what?"

"Yes. I'm going home to change and then I'm going back to work. A man's missing and I need to find out who and why. It's my job."

"Jesus, you're stubborn. The victim will still be dead tomorrow. It's after midnight now, and you almost drowned. What about that don't you understand?"

"You almost drowned? You okay now, Cora?"

"I'm fine, Mickey. He's a fussbudget. And you," she pointed at Kal, "Quit treating me like a child. What would I be doing if you weren't here? Answer me."

His harsh groan made Mickey laugh, and even she had to snicker.

His words held sarcasm, but not too much, "Then I'm going with you. Look, my hotel is closer. Let me out and I'll quickly change, grab the rental vehicle, and pick you up."

***

Once Cora stepped into her own shower, she could finally absorb the madness she'd just suffered. Feeling the water over her body yet again, she let loose all the emotions she'd kept hidden. The fear she couldn't release in public, the worry for her mother's loss if she'd have died and left her without her child, and the blissful gratitude to a man who braved the dark, cold waves to come to her rescue.

Her hero, the same guy who would curb her zany tendencies with smothered caring and lines not to be crossed. Did they stand a chance to be together? Him in New York. Her here in New Orleans. She couldn't leave her home or her mother? She didn't even know if he had ties that would keep him in his city. She hardly knew anything about him. Except that he'd snuck under her radar and had found a home in her sheltered heart.

Fuck!

Why now?

She washed her hair, scrubbing at her scalp as if to clear away her tormented thoughts. But they had control and wouldn't be scared off.

Kal might not have been aware, but she'd seen the way he'd fussed in her kitchen, lining up the mugs in her draining board like it mattered. What was that all about? Did he have a fetish for cleanliness, or was he just OCD about everything?

He wasn't OCD about jumping into the river tonight to save your skinny ass, now was he?

Son of a bitch!

***

Kal arrived, stepped into her living room to find Cora spiffed up in her too-tight black pants and a soft leather jacket over her white t-shirt, an outfit similar to the one he'd seen earlier. It wasn't the way the female agents in the bureau back home dressed, but these comfy clothes suited her perfectly.

She'd fluffed her hair all around her head as usual but had kept her make-up to a minimum. He liked it, liked her looking so competent. If he hadn't noticed the bruised look in her eyes, he would have kept his mouth shut.

"Cora, darling, come here." He moved close and put his arms around her body, not sure if he were stepping over some imaginary line, or he'd be welcome. "We don't have to go in. We can rest here until morning." She let him hug her. Though he sensed the stiffness, he gathered her closer until her body became pliant, and she relaxed in his arms.

"Let's grab a bite." He kissed her forehead. "We'll take a few minutes to eat and talk." He kissed her cheek. "Then, we'll tidy up the kitchen and head for the office." He kissed the softness of her arched neck. "Then we'll... Christ, what was I saying?" This time he kissed her waiting mouth and was lost. All thought flew out as passion took precedence.

He groaned his need. His hands gathering her in so he could feel her glued to him. He pushed himself against every part of her body, especially the groin area where satisfaction waited. Hunger took over, and he went with it.

Accepting her signals that passion had attacked her too, and she wanted him as much as he wanted her, he began to make love to her.

They kissed as if there were no tomorrow... only now, this moment, this reprieve. As if life now had a special meaning to them since they'd both faced death and beat it.

Their kisses became insane, each craving naked skin. They ripped at each other's clothes trying to help but were all thumbs and more in each other's way than the opposite.

Frustrated, stepping back from his hands, Cora stripped off her T-shirt and bra so he could see her beautiful breasts, full and white and pink nipples... calling to him. He left his own undressing and lifted his hands as if to touch the Mona Lisa, cautiously, delicately... adoringly. "You're beautiful. Perfect."

He looked into her watchful eyes and gulped. Tears had come over him without him ever knowing his body would betray him this way. He'd never been so involved with another person, never felt so filled with passion for anyone else. Having her matter so much, giving him her permission to see her perfection, her prideful way of saying without words – this is me. Are you willing to be with me, aware that I'm lowering barriers?"

He watched her eyes and saw her overpowered with emotion and instead of talking, he stripped off his own shirt and stood as naked as she was, stripped of pretention, mask off, his vulnerabilities exposed too.

"Do you want this... us? Now – tonight?"

"I've never wanted anything more."

"Me too, baby. Me too. Come here." He reached out his hand to help her make those steps and gathered her close. Once their bodies touched, the magic of earlier reappeared, and they kissed until he felt as if there was no Kal or Cora, no he or she – just them, together, melded... one.

She smoothed her hands over his back and to his hips, pushing at the jeans that still hampered her way. While he paid homage to her breasts, licking, kissing, and nuzzling the soft skin, she snuggled her face around his shoulders, to his cheek, wherever her lips could reach, biting and then kissing the tiny scars.

He couldn't stand any more, his knees weakened. She must have suffered from a similar ailment as together, they both lowered to the fuzzy rug underfoot.

Once there, he rolled to the side so he could strip off the rest of his clothes while she did the same. Within seconds, they were back in each other's arms, as if the parting were too much to bear.

"Come here, baby. I need you close." He scooped her under him, making sure he kept his full weight suspended by leaning on his elbows. They kissed yet again, both totally insane from having their bodies fused skin to skin.

He rubbed himself against her softness, reveling in the feeling and knowing she was as emotionally involved as himself. She arched upward and a consuming pleasure possessed him. Writhing wildly, she left him no misunderstanding of her need for him.

"God, Kal. Now. I want you now."

He loved the huskiness of her voice and thrilling words. No man could ask for more than to have the woman he most cared about want him so desperately.

"Yes, baby. I'm here." He caressed her body, leaving her breasts to reach lower and discover her wet welcome. *Jesus! How wonderful?* She was ready for him.

And he'd never been so fully engaged or engorged for any other woman. His body felt hot and full... and tormented. Trembling, hungry, he meshed with her, sinking into her hot loveliness, and felt as if he'd attained a fiery cloud in heaven.

Lordy... hot, drenched, she consumed him completely until he began to move forward and felt the tight pleasure of ecstasy from a woman's body not too experienced.

Slowly, carefully, he writhed his way inside, controlling his lust by gently caring for the woman who even now was kissing his neck and whispering lovely words into his ears. Words of encouragement for him to proceed, make her his, to keep doing whatever he was doing because she loved it, loved him.

Wha?

What did she say?

Her words made him crazy.

Wanting to please her more than he'd ever wanted to before, panting with hunger, he pumped into her body, moving this way and that, searching for the place where she most needed him to touch, to caress... to press.

As he delved deeper with each thrust, her gasps soon changed to tiny moans. Finally, she tightened around him and hung on, shuddering, convulsing, screaming sounds that made no sense, yet every lover knew they meant... "Oh My God!"

***

Not a virgin, but certainly not too active, Cora wanted this man, but other than showing him her needs, she left the lovemaking in his hands. After all, she ran every other aspect of her life with efficient bossiness, this was one area where she didn't have a lot of experience.

And it seemed that he did. Because he knew exactly how to touch her and where. How to drive her to heights she never knew were attainable with a lover who knew how to use his body to give pleasure.

Ensuring he'd made the experience pleasurable for her first, once she'd reached her peak and flew over, he drove into her for his own satisfaction. It came almost immediately, emphasized with words that kind of sounded like... "Oh, yeah," then followed up with groans, "so beautiful. You're beautiful."

Afterward, as their breathing slowed, along with their heartbeats, they lay together, wrapped in each other's arms, snuggling close. The tender intimacy cleared slowly and that's when the discomfort began to take shape. What was she doing?

She had a job.

There was a killer loose.

Breaking away from his arms, she began to dress.

Chapter
Twenty-nine

The material waiting for them at the New Orleans's police department shook Cora at first until they delved deeper. Turns out, their killer had a sense of humor, but also a weird respect for the law.

Someone had delivered a huge bouquet of flowers and they were waiting for her on her desk. A red satin bow and a card decorated the mass of colorful blooms. No one had touched the tiny envelope, but they were all loitering around wondering who'd sent their co-worker this incredible demonstration of affection.

"It's for me? You're sure?"

Freddie, Kal's partner, spoke first. "Uh huh, we checked. It says Detective Cora Taylor here... see?"

Cora moved in and pulled the card loose. She glanced at Hunter to see him watching, interested, seemingly happy for her to get such a prize. Having no idea who would send her flowers, she opened the flap and slid the card out. A cry escaped before she could reel it in, one of pure shock. Quickly, she held the edges of the little white piece of cardboard and lifted it so everyone could see what had been written.

You weren't supposed to jump into the river.

I'm sorry.

Kal quickly took a plastic evidence bag from his pocket and held it open so she could slip it inside along with the envelope. "You okay? You look shook up."

Cora knew she wore a dazed expression, hell she felt dazed. Never before had a criminal sent her an apology. Especially one in the form of a bouquet of flowers.

Freddie shook his head and added, "This dude is one weird actor. There's another piece of news that will light your birthday cake candles."

Cora laughed, the previous shock still affecting her. "What's that?"

"The man in the morgue wasn't one of the powerful guests, but a member of the staff. By the time we checked his photo against the database, we discovered he'd been an escaped convict. After his final trial, some of his pals highjacked the vehicle conveying him to the penitentiary. He'd been sentenced for life but had other plans."

"This better be good." Kal sat in one of the chairs and leaned back.

"Oh, it is." Freddie, center stage and in his glory, continued the lowdown on what they'd uncovered so far. "Four years earlier, when the transport truck carrying our victim to his new living quarters was attacked, one police officer was killed and the second man fatally wounded, but he'd lived long enough to tell the truth."

Cora, relaxed after handing off the evidence to a rookie to go to the lab for fingerprints, waited for Freddie's report to continue. "Which is?"

"Seems as if our suspect took a gun from one of his rescuers and shot his enemies, laughing hysterically the whole time. "Take that, cop!" were the words he'd screamed according to our sole survivor. Only, his aim had been slightly off, and that man had lived long enough to tell the tale. The assassin, one Ricky Burnett, had disappeared."

"Until tonight." Cora stood, engrossed by his criminal background. "You said this time around. What was he convicted of?"

Captain Larry Swanson, her immediate superior, arrived to answer the question. "He was to serve eight years for drowning his baby stepson amongst other atrocities. The guy was rotten to the core. He'd been in and out of jail all through his early years. His rap sheet looks like a script for a rerun of a Convicts movie. This time around, we suspect that he was running drugs on the Creole Queen. They found a huge stash in his cabin."

Cora commented, "Okay, that's harsh. What's

the story about his stepson?"

"Kid wouldn't stop crying. The mom had left him with Ricky, her boyfriend at the time, to go to work and came home to find his body on the bathroom floor. The coroner's verdict was death from drowning. The neighbor had called the cops because of the racket. Seems she heard him yelling for the kid to shut up and it finally did."

Cora shuddered. "The guy was real slime, wasn't he? Now I'm glad I didn't save his sorry ass."

Larry nodded, turned her way, and asked, his concern coming through clearly, "You alright? Heard about your late-night swim and figured that's a new one for you. I mean getting beaten, attacked, or wounded is more your norm. Having someone try to drown you should be added to the top of the list, you little maniac. How many times do I need to tell you to be careful, back off from being the hero?"

Kal straightened, his face a mask of anger. As if Larry understood the agent's involvement with his detective and sensing it wouldn't be prudent to push his agenda, he spoke as her captain, softly, almost sounding genial but meant every word. "You need to back off, spitfire. That's an order."

Cora chuckled and nodded. "Understood, Cap'n. And in case you wondered, I'm just fine."

Larry shook his head sadly. "Oh, Toots, what am I going to do about you?"

Kal, who'd watched the byplay, making sure

Cora wasn't in trouble with her superior, had been going over everything in his mind, working out what had happened to date. "You know, I just thought about something we might have missed in all our research. We've been so focused on the cold-case killer reenacting his earlier crimes that we've disregarded something important this time around."

Cora turned to the man who'd become too damn important to her and asked the question they all wanted an answer for. "What're you thinking, Hunter?"

Kal's eyes narrowed as he stared at her for a few seconds. She sensed he didn't like her referencing him as Hunter because that stripped him from lover status back to just being her partner. Too bad. She needed the reminder herself.

After Freddie cleared his throat, a sign for Hunter to continue, he became animated as he discussed his sudden revelation. "Think about it. This time, his victims have all killed. Heinous murders. Often with kids involved. We already understood our perp was finishing the job that justice had screwed up on, but it's deeper. He's like... like a vigilante, terminating the murderers themselves from our unresolved cases."

Cora understood exactly what he meant; they all did. "It's true. How many times have we caught the bad guy and given him over to the courts to either have them get released or sentenced with a ridiculous small slap on the hand, or worse... have them escape back into the world where we're forced to have to go after them again. It's fucking frustrating."

Listening carefully, Freddie now broke into the conversation with the one question no one could answer. "But... how does this assassin know about the earlier murders? And most important, how does he know about the people who need killing now, today... here in New Orleans?"

A whine followed his statement as if in agreement with asking the question. Shocked, Kal bent over to see a tail wag from under the desk.

"Jesus, Freddie. You brought Sam here tonight?"

"Look, man. He won't stay behind in the room. They've warned me once already not to leave him there because his howls piss off the rest of the customers."

Once he'd been found, Sam slowly advanced to Kal to lick his pointing finger and then turn his back as if to direct the attention back to Freddie. His ear pointed, his head turned, and Kal just knew he was waiting for the last question to be answered.

Freddie coughed away the chuckle they all saw on his face and continued with the earlier discussion, answering the question left hanging. "I've really given this a lot of thought. I've come up with a few answers, but I'm still puzzled. I suppose he could walk into police departments and see the

"Most Wanted" images on the wall. Or check the websites, or even earlier news reports. Maybe he's hacked into one of the databases? What do you guys think?"

Larry spoke his thoughts out loud. "Or he could be in a lowly position with the department that gets him privileges on the police computer programs."

Kal let his mind explore the information and asked, "But how did he know about the cases in New York?" As if the problem were more than he could handle at the moment, he slumped on the side of the desk and automatically reached out to stroke Sam's head. "My brain's sore from thinking about it. I vote we call it a night and work on the case in the morning."

As if his words were reacting on her body, Cora experienced an overwhelming exhaustion too, and knew she needed to relax her brain, maybe get some sleep, and start fresh the next day. The one area she refused to let her mind delve into was her breathtaking experience with Hunter.

Good intentions now firmly in place, she intended to head straight home. Suddenly, her phone's ringtone sounded, and earlier plans flew out the window. Truly, she had intended to call it a day.

But there was no putting off this caller.

Chapter Thirty

"Mom, what's up?"

"You were in the river? Almost drowned and you think I'm not going to find out. Hell, it's on every news channel. You know those reporters watch your comings and goings like hawks. They couldn't wait to fill the airways with your earlier notoriety, along with this new story."

"Look, I'm fine, Mom. I promise. I would have called, but it's after midnight. You should be asleep."

"So should you. Safe. In your bed. Hopefully with McHandsome. But nope, not my girl. She's off at some swanky ship party, taking a midnight swim to save a passenger. How can a mother sleep? You tell me."

"Shush, slow down and breathe. I'll be there to give you a hug, and you can see for yourself, I'm fine."

"You better bring your new partner with you. I have a few words I want to say to him too. And don't keep me waiting. An old lady needs her bed even if you young'uns can play around half the night."

***

"I'll just wait here in the car with Sam, Cora. You go in and put her mind at rest. Once she sees you're fine and gets those flowers, she'll back off... right?"

"Not a chance. Look, I told you I'd get home by myself, but oh no, the gentleman idiot from New York insisted on driving me. So now you can face the music too. She asked for you, and when she's riled, she's like a vicious coyote with a – a coon's leg in its mouth. If you think you can weasel out of getting a tongue whipping, you can think again. I'm not going in there solo. If there's two of us, she won't dump all the guilt on me."

Kal laughed. "Seriously, you have no trouble handling fistfights, men with guns, or cold rivers, but you balk like a seven-year-old when it comes to that lovely woman."

"That lovely woman has a viper's tongue and a whole shitload of contrariness she can't wait to share, so don't underestimate the enemy my friend."

Kal stepped out of the car after giving Sam the signal to stay and followed Cora up the cobbled sidewalk. It led them away from the front of the building to open patio doors on the left. The lights from inside flooded out onto the lawn.

He noticed the trees in the park area nearby and had to take a second look at the one in the forefront. An incredible, fully-grown Anseman Oak smothered in Spanish moss sat closest, spreading its meandering branches wide. What a gorgeous view for the resident.

He wondered if Cora's mom ate at the fancy table on the patio very often to enjoy the spectacular sight. Before he could ask, the woman herself flew towards them, her long, silky-blue flowered mumu-styled housecoat flowing around her as she attacked her daughter.

First, she hugged Cora as if she hadn't seen her for months, kissing her cheeks and patting her back, her arms tight and holding. "You're okay. Lord, child, you've never been a strong swimmer. Whatever possessed you to jump in that river?" Not waiting for an answer, she turned on Kal. "And you, where were you when she decided to act like a moron?"

Oh, oh! Cora sensed the tsunami before it flooded. Kal turned beet red, looking as guilty as an assailer caught with his hands all over the naked daughter.

Dawn, not being too dumb in the ways of the world, became delighted having caught the now terrified little mouse in her trap. Before she could make the most of this new situation, Cora cut in.

"Oh, no you don't. Leave Kal alone. It's too late to play silly games, Mom. I mean it. We're both fine but exhausted, so we're going home to bed, and you're going to settle down now and get some sleep."

"Going home to bed... you mean together? Pray God, it's true. Then I'll know he's heard my pleas."

Cora pushed over the bouquet of flowers, put her hands on her hips, and blasted Kal's laughing response to her mother's silliness with a cold stare before turning that same look on her mother. "Behave, Mummy Dearest. Go to bed. I love you. I'll see you tomorrow."

"Fine. But don't think these gorgeous flowers are going to get you off the hook." Dawn stepped down but added, "Good night you two lovebirds. Have fun together but do get some sleep." Then she swirled around, did a little shuffle while she carried her flowers inside, holding them like a precious baby. She closed the patio doors and shut off the lights, leaving Cora to face Hunter who stood waiting, watchful, and laughing.

"What's so funny?"

His expression instantly became solemn. "Nothing, baby."

"And don't call me baby. For God's sake, I'm a grown woman."

"Not to your mother. You're still her little baby and you always will be. Now you're mine."

***

Cora didn't know what to say after hearing his husky reply. So, she stomped over to the car and joined Sam. The question ringing in her head had to do with whether Kal's words held a special meaning.

And if he intended on staying with her for the rest of the night?

They really shouldn't be together – the department would frown on them having a romantic relationship. But he wasn't from New Orleans. He lived in New York. They could use that as a loophole if Larry decided to take a hard line with her and rake her over the coals, maybe demote her or even fire her.

She wished it were the biggest worry in her mind, but she knew instinctively her job would always be safe. As far as she could see, the major problem was whether that infuriating man was planning on leaving her alone or staying with her tonight.

God help him if he wasn't.

Chapter
Thirty-One

Kal drove Cora to her house and waited to see if she was intending on issuing an invitation or not. Once in the car, she'd snuggled her head on the window and never spoke except to give him directions when he asked.

He wanted to be invited... so badly. The thought of leaving her now drew his old inferiority complex to the forefront, the young-boy insecurities he'd hoped were healed... gone. Only, they weren't. He still needed some signal that she wanted him with her.

When she opened the passenger door without saying a word, he jumped from the vehicle forgetting to close his door. Being so involved, he didn't notice Sam right behind him.

"Cora, aren't you going to say anything?"

"What? I'm exhausted, and so are you. We need to rest."

"Okay, sorry. I'll see you in the morning."

"Hold it? Didn't you hear my mom?"

"She told us to get some sleep."

"She meant together, you idiot." Cora chuckled, delighted at seeing him redden again. Then she added, "Up to you." Cora waited for a few seconds and grinned along with him when he let her see the delight on his face.

He followed her into the house, Sam on his heels, and felt the nudge from behind. The dog was asking for water. He always stuck his nose in Kal's ass the same way every time he shared this particular revelation.

"Do you have any preferences for a specific bowl I can use for Sam? He wants a drink." Kal would never think to go into anyone's cupboards and help himself.

Cora laughed at Sam's naughtiness when she saw Kal jump. "Help yourself, the bowls are in the cupboard by the sink."

"But I might take the wrong one."

"No problem. It's just a bowl and can be put in the dishwasher." She went to the lower shelves, pulled out a silver container, and filled it with water. Then she lowered it to the floor. When Sam moved towards her, she patted his back and turned to Kal. "My bedroom is this way, and the couch is in the living room. Your choice."

Without waiting for his answer, she turned to the hallway. He heard her laugh when he tripped over the nearby chair to stay close and follow her. "Lord above, of course I'm coming with you."

"I hoped you would. But you need to know, I really do intend to sleep. I'm beat. So, no fooling around, got it?"

"Is snuggling allowed?"

"We'll see." She closed the bedroom door behind them, keeping Sam out.

Chapter
Thirty-two

She couldn't believe the man who'd jumped into the river to save her life could be so sensitive to her every mood, every word, watching for her signals. She'd have to back off from being so tough or she might scare him away.

This big, strong, handsome New York FBI agent was more sensitive than anyone she'd seen before. She'd watched the byplay in the kitchen and had known his worry about using her belongings was real. It mattered to him; therefore, it had to matter to her.

She went into the bathroom and slipped into the worn blue T-shirt that read Sexy but Cute she sometimes slept in. When alone, she preferred nothing at night, but she didn't want to tease. When she returned, he'd removed all but his Saxx underwear, black and fitting, of course, and watched as he headed to her bathroom. She hoped he'd see the new toothbrush still in the packet she'd left on the counter and not take offense or worry because it wasn't his brand.

She sensed the small chore like cleaning his teeth would be important. It had always been a big thing with her. Yet she didn't want to seem pushy. *Fuck, this relationship shit was a royal pain in the ass.*

Disgusted with her silly worrying, she opened her patio doors enough to get the fresh night air and climbed into her side of the bed, waiting, tense, and hating the feeling. In no time at all, Kal slipped in next to her and before she could feel uncomfortable in any way, he reached for her body, slid it in next to his, and wrapped both arms around her. "Sleep, baby. Sleep."

And sleep she did.

She'd never felt so safe, so warm... so loved. The night passed without the usual dreams she tended to suffer from after experiencing a dangerous situation. Tonight, the hours drifted, and it wasn't until she felt a strange hardness prodding behind her that she woke up.

Lying still for a few minutes, she realized that Kal's breathing had changed. He was also awake. She pushed against his body and heard his instant reaction. A ragged breath caught in his throat followed by a hoarse moan. "I'm sorry, sweetheart. I woke from a dream of us together, and my body responded. I want you so much, I couldn't control myself. But look, if you're tired, go back to sleep.

I'll behave."

"You might be able to sleep, but I'm an obedient daughter. I believe in listening to my mother's instructions." She laughed teasingly and turned into his waiting arms." I'm sure I heard her saying something about us enjoying each other."

"Funny thing, I heard the same." He leaned over her, his body hard and searching. His lips were oh... so tender as he tested to see if she would be welcoming.

Happy to accommodate his challenge, she opened her mouth and loved when he accepted the invitation and became totally focused on giving her what she craved.

His hands reached under her shirt and shimmied up her body, caressing each inch as he traveled to her breasts. Meanwhile, his lips took her straight to heaven. God, she was ready. The small amount of foreplay was all it took to get her back in the condition of earlier when they'd been together.

"Let me help you get more comfortable." He reached for the bottom of her nightie and slid it up and over her accommodating head. Then he took off his own briefs and moved closer, so they were body to body, lips to lips, fully in each other's arms.

Magic began building. Flooding with passion, she wrapped her arms and legs around his frame, giving him complete access. This time, she couldn't wait, didn't have the patience for him to get her ready when she was so close. She required him deep inside her now.

Seeming to understand her desperation, he readily complied, whispering the words she most wanted to hear. "Yes, baby. This is so beautiful, so.... beautiful. I love how you feel, how you make me feel."

His hands crushed her breasts together, kneading them gently, squeezing them with tenderness. His kisses traveled to her nipples, biting, licking, all while he pushed inside her, lifting her, impaling her, carrying her to heights higher than she'd ever reached – or ever thought possible.

Frenzied, she heard words bursting from her lips, words she couldn't hold in. "Yes. Like that. Hard, baby, hard. Oh, God. Yes-s-s." His penetration deepened until she thought she'd lose her mind from the ecstasy, the incredible passion.

Wanting him to feel the same, she tugged at his head so his lips were back on hers. Then she kissed him with such a deep frenzy that he moaned with pleasure.

Shuddering her climax, her body tightened around his and after a few more thrusts, she felt his release. They clung together for long moments letting the breathtaking intensity fade slowly.

He kissed her face, whispering his thanks. His hands smoothed her back and arms before he rolled over and tucked her in beside him.

"You're wonderful, you know that? A goddess."

She giggled and answered cheekily, "Forget it, Bud. I'm not gonna call you a God, so don't hold your breath."

"Okay, then, you're not a goddess. I'm sure those deities wouldn't whine and make little cries anyway, so there."

"I didn't cry or whine. I might have moaned a few times, but I draw the line at sounding like a baby."

Before he could answer, they both heard the cries again. And they were coming from under them.

Kal stiffened, rolled to stand on his side of the bed, and tripped over Sam.

Chapter
Thirty-three

It was Kal's swearing that had Cora scrambling for her T-shirt and turning on the light. Trying not to laugh at the spectacle of her naked man flailing on the floor with the huge, now happy dog, she couldn't stop the giggles.

"How did he get in? I know I closed the door so he wouldn't follow us."

Kal stopped struggling and sat with his arms on his knees. Sam now stood behind with his chin on Kal's head. Cora would swear the dog was laughing.

"Oh, right, I didn't warn you. Sam can open most any handle of any door that's unlocked. Even locked, he's managed to break in when he thought I was in trouble."

"We're you?"

"That's not the point. He knows better... stay is stay. But that doesn't seem to count with the brute." Kal rubbed his sore hip, put on his shorts, and turned to face his pet. "Wipe that grin off your face, Sam. You shouldn't be here. And what's with all the crying?"

"It's not him, Kal. I just heard it again, and Sam didn't make a sound." Cora slipped to the floor and looked under the bed. Close to where Sam had been lying sat a cowering bundle of white fur.

The minute the puppy saw Cora, she became ecstatic and flew to her idol. Sam left Kal to go towards Cora now holding the puppy at arm's length as if afraid to let it get too close.

"What the hell are you doing here, you little monster?" Cora couldn't believe that the puppy had found her. She must have gotten away from Mona's house and come all the way here in the dark... by herself.

As if the puppy knew she was in trouble, it began to shiver, and it stopped trying to lick Cora's face. Instead, it hung dejectedly in her hands.

Sam's growl started low in his chest. It was threatening. Cora sensed he had something to say and right now she was disappointing him. It was on her his narrowed gaze and snarling expression was focused.

Cora looked at Kal who stood still, his arms crossed and his expression carefully blank. He'd backed off, giving her the time he sensed she needed to make her decision. If she let the pup stay, there'd be no turning back.

Strangest thing she'd ever heard of – a puppy adopting her own mistress, but it seemed that this was the situation, and Cora had to make up her mind.

The rascal didn't move. She hung there like a limp little ball of fluff with black eyes to match her tiny nose... showing no animation, none. All it did was make soft little cries that could rip out a heart harder than hers.

This was the moment. Once she accepted the puppy in her home, she'd never be able to let her go again.

I am so screwed.

She lifted the puppy's face to hers. "Why me, you monster-mutt?"

Fitting into her hand easily, the baby stared adoringly at her, cocked her head sideways, and opened her mouth, flashing the cutest little smile Cora had ever seen.

Lord almighty, in one night she'd fallen in love with a big, strong male and a tiny, little female. *What fucking next?*

Using his nose, Sam nudged her warningly, and that's all it took. She snuggled the baby into her arms and lovingly kissed its head. Climbing back into the bed with her happy bundle, she turned to watch Kal point at Sam and then to the floor, "Lay down and stay."

Then the satisfied man got into the bed beside her to reach over and pet the now happy baby. A few seconds later, when Sam leapt on the bed to join them, she laughed at Kal's exasperation.

"He did what you said. He laid down, and he stayed. You just forgot to tell him how long."

Chapter
Thirty-four

Cora would have loved to stay forever in the bed with Kal and the dogs, but Larry's appearance put paid to that idea.

She quickly grabbed her fuzzy robe, put the puppy next to Sam, and went to let him in. "Stop banging so loud, you'll wake the neighbors for Chrissake."

Larry stood with a Starbucks holder and three coffees showing. Her eyes narrowed as she looked at his hands and then at him. "Why three?"

"I brought one for Kal too."

"What makes you think Kal's here?" Her sarcasm seemed ridiculous considering the circumstances, but it came out before she could hold back.

"You know, as I drove past to the coffee shop, I wasn't sure who owned the open-door car in the driveway, not until I saw the rental sticker on the back. Then it was a no-brainer."

Cora grumbled her answer, "It could have been Freddie's vehicle. Ever think of that?"

Larry laughed and ignored her peevishness. "Quit being a pain in the ass and go get dressed. We have to brainstorm today. There'll be another killing in the next forty-eight hours, and we need to change our focus and concentrate on the assholes who've gotten away with murder. And I mean that literally."

Kal appeared, holding the puppy who'd begun to fuss as soon as she saw Cora. He lowered her to the floor, and everyone stopped when she went into a crouch and peed on the rug by the sink.

Cora stopped, looked at Kal, and said, "Your cleanup. You let her down." Then she left the room laughing.

Kal took care of the mess before turning to see Larry's knowing grin. "Wipe that smirk off your face. What's the latest on the killer?"

"Freddie did more research, and we think we might know who the killer will be after next. You're idea of him only offing murderers was a good one. It narrowed our list down considerably."

"Who're the morons that are left?" Kal took a sip of his coffee and moaned with satisfaction. "Thanks man, this is good."

"Especially after doing a lot of exercise, right?"

"Screw you."

"Not your type, honey." Larry grinned

mischievously before clearing his throat. "So... the one person most likely to be of interest is Robbie Forrest. He's a psychopath that kills because he likes blood, preferably that of children. He caught up with two that we know of before we shut him down. I should say, Cora shut him down. And she put him away. Unfortunately, they only charged him with one manslaughter conviction. We didn't have enough evidence to get him for his earlier kidnapping and rape of a young girl they figured he was good for. Instead, the little girl's death we did charge him with, the body was found on his property." Larry shook his head at this point, disgust plain in his expression. "The sick bastard... we know he messed with her because he was sloppy and left a DNA sample."

"Seriously? You couldn't make it stick? What happened?"

"The silly coroner was new. She'd never handled a rape case before and made some irreversible mistakes. The lawyer fought to keep it out of the trial, and the damn judge who'd had a retrial situation to deal with at the time wasn't taking any more chances. Then the lawyer got the kidnapping charge thrown out since they were able to prove she'd gone willingly onto his property."

"What the hell?"

"She lived close by and was going after her dog when he caught up to her. Therefore, no kidnapping."

"But he held her against her will and killed her."

"Manslaughter. We found her naked body in an old well. He says he has no idea how she got there."

"She was naked? Why in the hell would she undress and then fall into the well?"

"See – that's exactly what we figured. But we couldn't prove he'd been the one to have undressed her."

"So, you couldn't prove he'd been the one to kill her."

"That's just it. Cora kept digging, she worked tirelessly to get that son of a bitch. She talked the judge into giving her a warrant, went to his place while he was at work and was able to find the girl's clothes under some floorboards. His hair sample showed up on the jeans."

"Then you had him."

"Nope. The fucking trial judge still wouldn't let us charge him with rape, we only got him on manslaughter. Every way you look at it, the tragedy was a series of sloppy police work and the asshole benefited. He served his seven years, and he's back walking the streets a free man."

Kal had his arms crossed tightly. The anger he felt ate away at his calm. "I understand why he's on the list now."

"Yeah– he got out about a month ago. We've been on his trail, watching his every move since then. Our boy has kept his nose clean so far, but we both know those tendencies won't just disappear.

Once we let up, he'll be back to his old tricks."

"Yet you can't put a tail on him forever. Jesus, sometimes I hate this job."

Cora entered the kitchen in time to hear the last bit of what Kal said. "Are you talking about Robbie Forrest? The psychopath that kills kids. He's the first name that hit me when Kal mentioned the type of people he figures our cold-case killer is after." She helped herself to the waiting store-bought coffee and looked first at Kal and then at Larry. "I know it's not allowed; I really get it... but I almost want to sit back, drink mint juleps, and wait for the inevitable. The assholes our killer is after deserve what he's handing out."

Larry started to speak, and Kal beat him to it. He had to know. "Can you? Sit back and let murder happen?"

Cora's eyes turned into shards of blue-ice. She stared at Kal, letting his words resonate, letting him see her resolve. "We're talking kids, bro. The fucker's lucky I didn't just shoot him the first time around. And before you say anything cute, I've never had trouble pulling the trigger again."

When she turned her eyes on Larry, she shrugged. "Let's go to the office and see what they've dug up about his pitiful dude, and then we'll round him up and play like good cops."

Chapter Thirty-five

By the time they'd dropped the puppy at Mona's, grabbed some takeout, and caught up with Freddie, who's smirking face said more about Kal not coming back to the motel the night before than he seemed prepared to put into words, Cora had her priorities in order.

Freddie had been busy. He found a few other maniacs who were suspects on the killer's list, and she took the printout to check what he'd come up with.

All of these dudes were sickos, a few were in the same gang and hung out together at one of the shoddy dumps in the French Quarter. They'd go there first and offer their warning before hitting on Robbie, the man she most hated for being the one who'd gotten away with such gruesome murders in her city.

"Let's go." Earlier, when she'd handed over the

little white rascal runaway, she'd switched out Mona's car for her jeep and was happy being behind the wheel again, Kal and Sam with her.

She drove past Bourbon Street, not near as vibrant as the night before when the liveliest place in town provided ongoing parties for all the excited visitors, including jazz music that spilled out onto the streets, fancy drinks in ridiculously large holders, and Cajun food to die for.

Heading into the slummy area toward the clubhouse the losers chose as their cave, she pulled up in front, watchful for any guns being trained on them.

These guys didn't play around. They were the real deal, mobsters to the core. None of them had any compunction about killing a cop and hiding a body, hell they'd done it before more than once. Hid the officers so well, they'd never been found. And with no body or witnesses, it's almost impossible to charge someone for murder and make it stick.

Cora held Kal back and passed on her warning. "These guys don't play games. They'd just as soon shoot you as look at you, so don't make any sudden moves or play tough. Any reason at all is enough for them to react."

"Got it. Can we bring Sam?"

"I guess. Just control the dog. Don't want them to think he's a threat and shoot him."

"Okay. Let's go. How about I take lead this time."

Before she could answer, Kal stepped ahead of her and entered the front door of the place.

***

He felt the eyes of all five men sitting at one table on him immediately. The fat, bearded bartender lifted his rifle and laid it on the rough wood counter, and then continued to wipe his stack of glasses as if the morning hadn't just become interesting. The half-dressed waitress hovering near the bar turned her back as if she didn't want to be recognized.

Since it was just mid-afternoon, the other customers milling around were low-key, gambling, or passed out. The stench of the various gatherings housed here – everything from beer to cigarettes and spilled liquor to marijuana hung in the murky air.

Kal sensed Cora coming into the darkened place behind him and was glad she'd let him take lead. He'd read the files earlier and had a good picture of the main bosses around the table. He sauntered up to the oldest he'd recognized as the leader and smiled; all were armed and two were holding their weapons in their laps.

"Sorry to barge in like this, Mr. Fernando, but I have a message for you and your men. Figured to pass it on in person."

Fernando smiled evilly, seeming to get a kick out of the situation. "What's up, officer?"

"Actually, It's Special Agent Hunter. I'm with

the FBI, here on assignment from New York. Seems there's a serial killer on the loose, and we're thinking he might be coming to your establishment to take a few lives, probably yours and maybe others who work for you."

"Is that so?"

"Yep. Fraid it is. This fellow has a vigilante complex and goes after people who've broken the law and gotten away with it, especially those who've killed. He's hit New York numerous times and has recently arrived in New Orleans to carry on his spree here."

The older man at the table, head full of gray hair fashioned in waves and mustache groomed to twirl at each side, seemed to get a kick out of his uninvited guests. A mob boss who surrounded himself with bodyguards and reliable lawyers, he laughed, and the others followed. His expression became amiable as if he were enjoying the diverting performance.

"What makes you think he'll come after a nice-a guy like me. I'm-a no killer."

"Yeah, tell that to the judge."

Fernando glanced over at Cora who'd hung back, leaning against one of the pillars, Sam beside her. "Hey, Cora. Nice to see you again."

"The privilege is all yours, Fernando. I'm here to do my duty and warn you about the man we think might come for you. Watch yourselves, this guy is as serious as poison."

Sam had stood when she began to speak, but he didn't move away from Cora, just remained watchful and waiting.

Kal turned his back to the men at the table as if to move closer to Cora and spoke loudly. "They've been warned. Let's go."

He didn't see the man push the chair under his feet to trip him and neither did Cora. Sam, on the other hand, saw it all and his growls were enough for the men lounging at the table to jump back, some stood and jerked away, two chairs fell over.

The only ones who didn't flinch were Fernando... and Kal who'd managed to step around the fallen chair rather than trip over it.

He looked at the idiot who'd made the move and spoke low, his tone conversational rather than confrontational. "Can't help yourself, huh?" He motioned to the dog. "Sam. Here."

The dog approached his side and waited, his fangs showing business. His quivering body in attack stance.

Kal turned to Fernando. "You should train your boys better."

Fernando shrugged, his manner insolent. "Well, you know, boys-a will be boys. By the way, what does this assassin look like? I'll get my guys to be extra vigilant."

Kal chuckled. "Nobody knows. All we have on this zealot is he's a male, medium height and white. Call if you have any trouble."

Fernando nodded. "Sure. I'll call for you to come and pick-a up the body if he tries anything stupid."

"Right, you do that. In the meantime, drink up and enjoy the time you have left."

Kal headed toward Cora and let her go in front of him out of the bar, Sam on his heels.

Once on the sidewalk, he chuckled. "Nice way of telling them about the poison."

"I thought so too." Cora laughed. "I kinda thought we should warn them about the killer's probable MO for this assassin." She winked at him and added, "I liked your reference for them to drink up."

Kal shrugged, put his hands in his pockets, and followed her to the jeep. "I was trying to be a nice-a guy."

Cora laughed and headed to the driver's side.

Kal stopped dead. His instincts on high alert. He was pretty sure that Cora didn't see the man hovering at the corner of the building, but he did. "Wait here." He expected her to obey and was thrilled when she did.

He walked slowly over to the fellow who'd gestured at him. "What's up?"

The forty-year-old Mexican, who looked like he'd come through some rough times, spoke; his voice low and urgent. "You a cop?"

"FBI. Agent Hunter. What can I do for you?"

"Fernando has a half-dozen girls in the backroom, girls they were intending on shipping out to the west coast, but the truck broke down, and they were brought here. My daughter is one of them."

Kal stared into the pock-marked face and frantic eyes of the terrified man and asked, "You know this how?"

"I followed them when they took my Maria."

"Okay, look, don't fight me. Act drunk and keep your head down." Kal reached for the man's arm and frog-marched him toward the jeep, pretending to arrest him.

While he added the cuffs, making it appear real, he told Cora what he'd just heard. She nodded and made Sam move over so they could push their hostage into the back seat. She whispered. "Don't worry. We'll help you. Come with us now, and we'll return with a S.W.A.T. team."

Chapter
Thirty-six

By the time they had assembled the team and were ready to hit the bar, an hour had passed. Cora felt tight with worry and would have gone in there herself if Kal and Larry hadn't pulled rank and made her step down.

Larry reminded her, "Cora, settle down. You know I sent a squad car to be sure they didn't take the girls out of the place. We need to be careful if we're going to make this arrest stick, you know that. I want it done by the book."

"How fucking much longer is it going to take? For chrissakes, those bastards could be hurting those girls while we're playing at getting it right."

Kal appeared and offered, "I'll go with you, Cora. Mr. Becerra, Maria's father, just confirmed there were at least a half dozen girls. A couple of them worked together and had met up with this bogus studio entrepreneur thinking they were going to get parts for a new TV series. Instead, they were kidnapped and brought to New Orleans. His daughter had told him about this wonderful opportunity, but he hadn't believed in miracles. Instead, he followed her and saw what actually played out, so he knew where they'd stashed the girls."

"He's a good father but it must have been daunting as hell to know they had his girl, while he could do nothing. When did this happen?"

"Two nights ago. He told me they'd all met at some crap studio, signed the papers, and were taken in a fancy van to a motel. That bothered him, so he snuck up to the room and watched through the blinds as they put the plastic tie wraps on the girls and covered their mouths with duct tape. Just as he'd decided to leave long enough to find a cop, an old delivery truck showed up. It was the middle of the night, and they were able to get the girls transferred without anyone the wiser and drove them to Orleans."

"He followed. It must have been horrifying for the poor man."

"Yeah. He had no cell phone, no way of contacting anyone, he just stayed on their trail. When they pulled into a gas station close to the city, the driver and his sidekick went into the convenience store, and he managed to add two large bottles of cola to their gas tank. He prayed it would force them to stop."

"Good for him. It must have done the trick."

"Yeah, they made it this far and decided to bring their shipment here while they sorted out the damaged vehicle. We happened to pull up for our interview around the same time as they were unloading the girls in the back."

Cora gritted her teeth. Her normally pretty blue eyes revealed shards of black. "Good, see... there is a God."

***

They arrived at the bar and parked a block over, waiting until the S.W.A.T. team were in place and ready to go in. The team leader gave three of the men directions to cover the back of the clubhouse while the other three stayed with them.

The two officers ordered earlier to watch the area joined them, one came from the back of the building where he'd been in hiding, and the female officer from the unmarked police car also met with them as backup.

Kal gave the order for Sam to stay, and he followed Cora's vested figure with blazing yellow NOPD slashed across the back to the entrance. Wearing his own FBI protection, he lifted his gun at the ready, checked to see that the men were in place, and stepped forward into the nightclub.

Awaiting them was the most shocking sight they could ever have imagined.

Chapter
Thirty-seven

Cora couldn't believe the change from earlier. Instead of the five men sitting comfortably at the table, enjoying the cards and their beer, five men still at the table were dead... all face down.

The waitress lay in a mound on the floor, terrified, crying hysterically, a broken glass next to her. The bartender, looking shocked as hell, put down the phone. "I was just calling you guys. There's been a murder – five to be exact."

Kal looked at Cora and saw the same shock he couldn't hide. "Do you believe this?"

She looked at the five bodies, all appearing as if they died instantly and shook her head. "That's just nasty."

Suddenly the waitress began to gag as if she were fighting for breath and Cora went down beside her. Frantically, the waitress tried to stick her finger in her mouth to make herself vomit.

It was the broken glass that gave Cora a clue and she just knew the worker had been given a drink but hadn't actually swallowed enough to kill her instantly. Otherwise, she'd be as dead as the others. Yet the signs were clear that she'd maybe had the glass to her mouth.

Yelling the order for them to call for an ambulance, she quickly hefted the girl up and wrapped her arms around her waist, so her upper body hung down, and shook her hard. Within a few seconds, the poor girl was able to upchuck and clean out her guts.

Helping the poor girl to the chair, Kal had moved close, she sat her down and then crouched nearby. Wiping the poor girl's face with the napkin Kal handed her, she asked the question they all wanted answers for. "What the fuck just happened?"

Chapter
Thirty-eight

It was hours later that Kal was able to relax at the office with Freddie, Larry, and Cora. All were exhausted yet feeling a strange euphoria for having to deal with dead bodies of people whose passings weren't breaking their hearts.

He glanced at Cora who sat on the floor beside Sam, the dog's head in her lap, his face a picture of ridiculous bliss with his tongue sliding over the side of his teeth as he panted his enjoyment.

Larry answered the call that came to his cell, listened, and hung up with a quick thanks. "You did good, recognizing the signs of poisoning with the waitress, Cora. She's awake and willing to talk. Maybe you and Kal can go see her at the hospital, get her statement, and then go grab a few hours off, maybe get a bite. I have a feeling it's going to be a long night."

Cora caressed Sam's floppy ear. "All that fucking

paperwork. But you know something I thought I'd never say... I kinda don't mind filling out the forms for those departed bastards."

"You and me both, Rookie." Larry turned to Freddie to ask a question.

Kal watched Cora carefully separate from Sam and everything in him wished he could have changed places with Sam to have her hands all over him. Driving the image from his mind, needing to control his body from misbehaving, he headed for the door and waited with it open.

Both Cora and Sam headed his way and the vision hit him like a sledgehammer to his gut. They looked so damn good together. He turned before the sudden, overwhelming emotion became visible.

They all headed to the jeep and for the rest of the drive to the hospital, his mind wandered, filled with his new problem, and looking for solutions.

God help him, the last assassination was scheduled to happen in two days. Then as long as everything went down the same way it did ten years earlier, he'd be free to return to New York soon after. Put all the wonderful heat, friendly faces, and... his new ladylove behind him.

Could he leave Cora and go home to New York when the job was done? It's where he'd lived all his life. His mother still occupied the same apartment in Queens, and being a tenacious sucker for right and wrong, the guilt of leaving her alone would ride him constantly.

After all, it's what his dad had done. He'd committed suicide when Kal was an adolescent, leaving his mother to bring him up. And she'd done a good job, giving him a comfortable, secure, and loving home.

But he'd never forgiven the man who'd let him down... ever.

His feelings ran deep. If his father had loved him, loved his wife, why would he have left them? He wasn't sick or depressed or in financial difficulties. He'd had a loving relationship with the man as had his mother. There were no gray areas in this equation, not for Kal. It was pure black and white. You love your family, you hang around.

You kill yourself... who do you love more?

Now here he was in a spot where he faced a decision. How could he ask Cora to leave everything she'd known all her life, the astonishing heat, the place where everyone knew her, to move to the colder climate, and it wasn't just the weather, but often the inhabitants' attitudes residing in The Big Apple.

Positive she'd get a job without any difficulties, he had to admit to feeling his worry spike when he thought of her working in what could be a nightmare of violence in a city that never stops.

Once they reached the hospital, he let go of the worries. When she asked her question, he realized she'd sensed his mind wandering and had backed off to give him room. Goddamn, he appreciated a woman who had the wisdom to know when a man needed quiet.

"You okay, Kal?"

"Just a few decisions I was thinking over, nothing to worry about, baby." He walked close enough to take her hand and squeeze gently before dropping it.

"Figured you had something on your mind, I could almost hear the squeaky wheels turning as my mom used to say. Whatever thoughts you were working on, they must have been some powerful." She laughed to show she was teasing but he heard the slight worry she'd covered with the joke.

What a lucky man he was to have found such a gem, one who cared so deeply for him. No way could he let her down, give her up... not now. Not ever. He wasn't his old man, no matter how often the thought worried him in the past. He'd finally found someone he cared about more than himself, and he'd never leave her of his own free will.

Ever!

Now he'd just have to explain his new purpose to his mom and beg her to make a change. He'd get her a place next to Cora's mom, Dawn.

He'd do anything...

Chapter
Thirty-nine

Cora worried about Kal's silence in the jeep, yet she sensed she shouldn't chatter to fill in the silence. Didn't she hate it when others did that to her? Instead, she left the radio playing low and enjoyed the streets of her city, the place she loved. Was her time here coming to an end? Would there be a confrontation about the next step in their relationship, or would he just leave and go back to New York?

The thought made her feel ill.

When they arrived at the hospital, she questioned him because it seemed like the right thing to do. Make sure he didn't need anything, especially from her. It's what a friend would do, and she felt a lot more than friendship for the man. His smile and the tender way he let her know she mattered went a long way to wrapping up any doubts she might have tried to manufacture.

After all, she'd never had a close relationship that threatened her way of life before. No one had ever come close enough to even make her heart tremble let alone flip over in surrender.

They found the waitress's room, a woman by the name of Star Bolin. When they entered, the nurse looked up and upon seeing their badges, she nodded, patted the hand of the pretty black female, and left.

Cora stepped forward first and reached the bed where the big brown eyes of the girl had latched onto hers. They filled once they recognized Cora as the one who'd come to her aid by the bar.

Impulsively, she reached out, the gesture meaningful and she seemed relieved when Cora gathered it in hers and leaned in close. "Thank you for helping me earlier. I-I have a little boy who I couldn't bear to leave. So, you know, he's why I'm even in that horrible place. The pay is nothing, but the tips keep a roof over our heads."

"Hey, I'm no judge, honey. We do what we must to survive. I'm just thrilled you're okay. Can you tell us what happened earlier, what you remember?"

"Sure. The guys, behaving in their usual way of brainless assholes, were all worked up about some shipment they hadn't expected to come to the clubhouse. I heard something about vehicle difficulties, and they were forced to stop driving. I didn't get a lot of the conversation, because frankly, I try not to listen. Around there, knowing too much can get you killed."

"Smart girl. Then what?"

"Turns out, they had a party in mind and were working on getting high and stupid so they could enjoy themselves. I mean, seriously, they were giggling like a bunch of high-school freaks when Fernando ordered his favorite bottle of Tequila."

"Tequila? For shooters?"

"Yeah, they all like to down shooters to celebrate and a new bottle had somehow appeared on the bar. Have no idea how it landed there, the bartender asked me if I'd taken it down from the shelf where they usually store it, but I hadn't touched it."

"Yet he opened it?"

"Yeah. Sometimes the guys like to make a gift to the boss, and they leave him an expensive bottle of his favorite booze. No doubt, Jimmy at the bar just figured it was another present. So, he opened it, put it on the tray with a bunch of glasses – some of those jerkoffs like to break them after they down the first drink – and I brought the tray to the table." Star looked at Cora and then toward Kal. "I can't be charged for bringing it to them, can I? I had no idea there was anything wrong with the stuff."

Cora squeezed her hand. "Of course not, Star. The only one responsible is the person who placed the Fentanyl in the bottle and brought it to the bar knowing it would get used. So, you brought the tray, and they poured the shots. How did a glass come to you?"

"The one pouring the shots, Joey, has a thing for me. I keep putting him off, but he never stops trying. He played bartender for the table, and he filled a glass for me. They all laughed. As if it was a big joke. When they lifted the glasses to drink, I went to lift mine, and at that exact moment, a drunk customer stumbled past and pushed my arm just as I'd lifted it to my mouth. Only a very tiny amount touched my lips, but it made me sick enough... that and watching everyone else dying. It was horrible, a – a ghastly nightmare."

"No doubt it was. I'm sorry you had to have seen it. But so you know, the shipment they were talking about wasn't drugs. It was a van filled with young girls they'd kidnapped and were taking to some buyers lined up out west. Do you know anything at all about that?"

Shocked and showing it, Star burst into tears. "You gotta believe me, ma'am, I knew nothing about any girls. Hell, I'da called the cops myself if I'da known. I lost a sister to those trafficking creeps a few years back. I'da never stood for that kind of shit going down."

Cora grinned as she calmed the patient. "Relax, Star, no one thinks you had anything to do with that shipment or their business dealings."

Star nodded and slowly laid back against the pillow. "You know what? I worried I'd be having nightmares about what happened today, but now, I don't believe I'll be haunted at all. As soon as I feel any remorse for those bastards, I'll think of those girls and how terrified they must have been, and how lucky they were that the men never got to have their fucking party."

Cora chuckled along with Kal. "Works for me too, Star. Sometimes God has a sense of humor. In this case, he arranged for them to die before they could make the girls pray for their own deaths. It's the kind of sweet justice I can handle. Just wondering, did you get a look at the customer who saved your life?"

"No. Everything happened so fast. He mumbled an apology and stumbled out the door. From the quick glance I gave him, I know he was white, wore a tuque, and wasn't one of the regulars I'd recognize. Within seconds, the guys started gagging and dying, and I freaked out. Then you showed up."

Kal leaned in and asked, "Did you know your video machine was on the blink?"

Star blew her nose on the tissue she grabbed from the rolling side table and gave him her attention. "That piece of junk is always getting replaced. If they'd buy the better product, maybe they wouldn't have so much trouble. Jimmy can probably help you more with information about that."

"Yeah, we have him downtown right now. The

guy's totally bummed, can't believe what he saw. Says he knew nothing about the shipment either."

"You can believe him. We've had plenty of talks where he's told me to keep my eyes and mouth shut about anything I might hear or see in the place. It was healthier. I'm pretty sure he did the same. Besides, I'd almost swear they've never brought any merchandise anywhere near there before or we'd have seen it."

Cora stood up and put her hand on Star's cheek. "I'm glad you're feeling better. You need anything, you call. I know how tough it can be out there sometimes."

Star sadly nodded and then perked up, her cheekiness amusing. "You know anyone who'll hire a really good worker who has a juvenile record and a special-need's kid?"

Cora smiled. "Sure do. I mean it, Star. You need a new job where you won't be around scum like that, you let me know. I have a friend who owns a Care Home for seniors, and they always need girls who have big hearts and care about others. Here's my card."

Star's hand trembled noticeably as she reached out to take the offering. "I'll call." Her voice shook with an emotional tone. "As soon as I get home."

"Good. I'll set up an appointment for you with the Director. She's good people. Take care."

Chapter
Forty

Kal had never felt prouder of anyone than he did about the woman who walked beside him, her head level with his shoulder and her heart bigger than the jeep they approached.

"That was a nice thing you did for Star. I bet you left her feeling better than she has in a long time. And a new job prospective, what's with that?"

"If she actually takes advantage of the offer. Some don't, unfortunately. I happen to know that the home where Mom lives is always looking for girls to start working there. Many of them stick around, but you know younger girls who are still trying to find a future decide to go on to a nursing career or physical therapy, even yoga instructors. Hell, once those old biddies, and I'm talking men and women, get through with those innocents, they've set them on new pathways to build a better future."

"You sound like a slogan."

"Yep, word for word. Mom organized a trust fund where a lot of them donate money toward giving some of the workers a scholarship so they can afford to move on. I think Star would be perfect for them to help out."

"And I think you're perfect for me to take out for a late dinner. How about some Jambalaya and jazz?"

"I know the perfect place."

In no time at all, they were seated close to the stage where a group of musicians were making magic happen with their instruments. The piano player must have taken a potion because his fingers flew across the keys so the others with the horns had no choice but to give their best. The fellow on the saxophone tried his hardest to outdo his compatriot, but the pianist wouldn't stop, and the place stood to their feet in appreciation. Cora beside Kal applauded and hooted too, calling out a name and clapping with glee.

They settled down while the band took a break, and their food was delivered. "This is spectacular." Kal loved the well-seasoned dish, and being starved, he didn't hesitate to fill up. Funny thing, he'd finished eating before it dawned on him that he hadn't worried about the placement of the cutlery or whether the table was cleaned sufficiently.

All those OCD habits he'd picked up somewhere in his early years had started to fade in importance next to the woman at his side and the desire to impress her rather than show too many weaknesses.

She finished off her bowl and pushed it aside, then gave him a grin before she spoke. "You know, I've been thinking about Star's close call. And... about my own experience in the water and having an angel push me to the surface so I wouldn't drown. Do you think they could be the same?"

Kal thought over her words. They made sense. "You're saying you think the drunk at the bar could have been the killer, making sure an innocent didn't die from his poison."

"You're right... it's hard to fathom. A killer with a heart. He must have grown one over the last ten years because he sure as shit didn't do things like this back then."

"A man can change over that period of time. Remember, he stopped his bizarre splurge of murdering strangers for no reasons we ever found."

"True. Makes a strange kind of sense, right? I mean, the killer sent me flowers. And now that I think about it, there was a huge bouquet in Star's room." Suddenly, Cora pulled out her phone and made a call.

As soon as she hung up, Kal questioned, "You sent officers to check out Star's flowers to see if there was a card, right?"

"Yeah. I think if she'd have gotten one, she'd

have mentioned it, unless she thought they came from someone else. Better to be safe than sorry. They *were* in her room."

Before Kal could comment further the piano player approached the table and Cora stood with her arms wide open and waiting. "Louis, my friend. You didn't let me know you were going to be in town."

"I was gonna, baby. Just got here this morning."

"And you couldn't stay away from the joint." She hugged him again and then pointed at the free chair next to Kal's. "Come and have a beer with me and my partner from New York, Special Agent Kal Hunter."

The men shook hands, and Louis, a young, good-looking man with a glint in his dark eyes, gave Kal a once-over that didn't mess around. Serious as sin, he looked deep into his eyes before he nodded his approval and let go of Kal's hand. "My girl here's good people. Ya'll better be nice to her or you'll be in deep shit with me and the boys. Ya hear?"

"Sure do. She's special. You got my word."

"Good." Louis turned to Cora, his eyes now pleading. ". Sing for me and the boys."

"I'm rusty as hell, Louis. Haven't been up there for ages."

"Then it's time for you to have some fun. Come on. The crowd will go wild, let's give them a treat."

Kal turned to her, his expression questioning.

She grinned at Louis and then answer the unasked question. "Ever heard of garage bands? We formed one when we were in our teens. Louis and the boys stuck with their music, and I veered off to become a cop."

Louis added, "Every once in a while, if we're lucky, we can talk her into coming up on the stage with us for old times sake."

Kal had no time to filter through what was happening before Cora touched his arm reassuring him, took Louis's hand and they both stepped up on the stage. He watched as the other three in the group all greeted her with hugs and kisses, obviously thrilled to see her up there with them.

Before the shock could wear off, the rest of the room, especially those working at the bar and the servers, all went wild when they saw who'd joined the band. They began throwing out song choices and the one that hung in the air the most was the song they began to play.

Cora held the mic in her hand as if she'd been born with one and she leaned on the piano looking toward Louis as he played the introduction.

One of Kal's favorite records passed on from his father was Louis Armstrong and Ella Fitzgerald's Summertime album. When the first notes of that song broke the silence, he stiffened. Then he prayed that his Cora sang the notes even close to the way one of his favorites could.

From the beginning, the room, quiet now, was

entranced. In awe, he listened to the wonderful song soar from the mouth of a natural who was born to be on stage. Why had she chosen the life of a cop when talent oozed from her body like God's special handiwork?

He watched her sing to Louis, forcing him to perform along with the song, making his piano hit the notes to bring tears, supporting her voice rather than just taking over. It was a precious moment in his world never to be experienced again.

But to be cherished as a sweet memory of the night his heart filled with her voice, joined her body... never to return.

He was in love.

With one of God's special gifts to the world.

The weight of responsibility doubled because he knew he'd always watch over her, protect her, and love her till the day he took his last breath. He was his mother's son... not his father's. He'd never leave her. How could he? He'd be crippled worse than he already was... and she'd still hold every tender feeling he'd ever feel again for the woman he loved.

Once the song finished, the crowd roared for more. Cora laughed and took a seat next to Louis to play a silly melody on his piano. Before they could decide what to perform next, she pulled out her cell and checked the message, which put an end to the impromptu performance. Seeing what was happening, Kal left sufficient money on the table for the bill and stood waiting.

Kissing Louis and blowing more smooches to the boys, Cora headed to the door and waved for him to follow.

What now?

Chapter
Forty-one

Cora had never passed on this kind of message before, especially to someone she loved. Wanting to be as sincere as she possibly could, she waited until they were near the jeep to answer his query.

"Cora, what's up?"

"It's your mom, Kal. Freddie sent me a text, asking me to break the news to you. She's had a heart attack. He said it's not too serious, she's conscious and the doctors are optimistic for a full recovery, but right now she's fragile, and she's asking for you."

Kal grabbed for the jeep's rollbar. "Jesus, a heart attack? The woman's never sick. I don't remember the last time she even went to the doctor." Kal propped himself against the vehicle and Sam, sensing a problem, was beside him instantly, putting his big head on Kal's shoulder. For a dog that seldom showed emotion, he whined sorrowfully as if he recognized his owner's pain.

Cora moved close and leaned her body against his on the opposite side of Sam. If the animal thought it important for Kal to feel the touch from those who cared, she'd play along. Waiting, not moving, she let him absorb the hit. She knew how she'd feel if something like that happened to Dawn.

"I have to go."

"Of course, you do. I'll drive you to the hotel to get your things and then to the airport."

"But how can I leave? If things go as planned, the killer will strike again the day after tomorrow. I don't want you approaching that bastard, Robbie Forrest, alone."

Cora stiffened, not sure if she was insulted at his lack of faith in her ability or pleased because he was being protective. This fucking love shit could sure mess with a girl's head and fill it with doubts. Rather than taking his comment the wrong way, she asked for an explanation. "Not sure what you mean? I can handle him, you know that."

"There's no doubt in my mind that the guy will lose if he tries anything, but he's a psychopath, and you have a heart. The scenario is mighty unbalanced in my book. Promise me you'll have backup."

Pleased with Kal's explanation, she answered softly, "I promise. Hell, I'm not even sure we'll be able to track him down after they lost his trail.

Freddie's been on it for the last two days and still doesn't have an address. Look, your mom needs you. You don't really have a choice."

"I know. I have to go to her. She's a sweetheart, raised me all by herself after my prick of an old man took a bottle of pills, and backed out of the whole scene."

"Lordy, I'm so sorry, Kal." Cora leaned her head against his shoulder, moving in even closer than before. If she could have lifted him into her arms and held him like one would a hurt child, she'd have done so in a heartbeat. So, this is love – feeling another's pain viscerally, as if it were your own.

She sensed him taking solace in her behavior. It helped that she mattered when he needed a friend. In no time, she delivered him to his hotel. He looked at her from the passenger seat, Sam's head still resting on his shoulder. "I have a bit of time. It's going to be a couple of hours before my flight. Come with me, I need a few minutes alone with you."

She didn't answer, just nodded, and followed him up the stairs to his room, making space for Sam to walk beside them. Once the door to the room was closed, he turned and swept her into his arms, kissing her as if he couldn't get enough of her taste.

She had no problem with his actions, she felt the same, wanting him to know how much he mattered, yet not being able to put her feelings into words... not yet. Shy in this one area, she used her lips and arms to tell him how important he was to her.

Within moments they were mostly undressed and on his bed, making love to each other with frantic moves, deep kisses, and sensitized bodies needing fulfillment. Fast, hard, he entered her and they both lost their battles with sanity as they drove each other wild. Was it his imminent departure, their coming separation that added to the frenzy? Cora had no way of knowing his emotions.

For her, it was the awareness of him leaving her and not knowing when she would see him again. The loneliness had already started seeping into her awareness, and he hadn't even left yet. He'd become so important in her world, that facing his departure was worse than coming up against a lunatic with a gun. She'd know exactly what to do then. But now, she had to follow his lead and hope she didn't break down in a pitiful mess or hang onto his leg when he went to departures at the airport.

While he showered and quickly dressed, she called Freddie to let him know about their arrangements. His voice left her no doubt that Kal mattered. "He'll be sad to leave. I know him. Not a lot would take him away from this case. It's been on his agenda for ten years, his and Shawn Bonaire's. He was Kal's old partner before he retired."

"Were they together very long?"

"Oh, sure... years. Like an old married couple from what I've heard. More than one source told me that Kal was heartbroken when Shawn inherited a bundle and turned in his badge early. I've been working with him since, and he's a hell of an agent, but shall we say, it's been difficult to get close. He's a good guy. He'll do what's right."

"He has no choice, says his mom brought him up and taught him the rules. They seem pretty close."

"She raised him, and he adores her. Can't imagine how he feels. I'm just thankful the doctor's reports on her condition are good. Yet they admitted she probably won't settle until he arrives."

"His flight leaves at midnight and he'll be there by morning. Look, did you get any leads on Robbie, yet?"

"No. But I found his brother. Took me a while to convince him we weren't looking to make any arrests. He said he was going to talk to Robbie and let me know tomorrow where he might meet up with us."

"Good. At this point, I almost don't care if we're in time to give him a heads-up. He's such bad news; it seems like a karmic joke for the law to give a rat's ass about him meeting his maker."

Freddie's chuckles came through clearly. "True, but informing the bastard about his pending flaming demise kinda tickles my funny bone."

Laughing along with Freddie, Cora agreed. "Well, when you look at it that way, I have to agree. Whenever we get the directions, I'll need you to come along for the ride."

"I'm your guy. Look forward to it. I'll get my water pistol filled. Bye."

As soon as Kal finished getting his backpack ready, he smoothed the wrinkled mess on his bed and set out the water and food for Sam. Sighing like a man regretting his mission, but determined to carry on, he stiffened his shoulders and turned to send her a wink.

"Okay, baby. I'm ready."

Cora lowered her phone and grinned. Watching her big bad FBI agent measuring the quilt to make sure it was even on both sides tickled her funny bone. His indulgence for Sam regressing into huge hugs put a lump in her throat.

"Let's get out of here." He moved to the door, holding it open for her. When Sam began to follow, he gave the signal for the dog to stay and closed the door. They headed for the stairs. Before they'd moved ten feet the racket from the annoyed animal could wake the dead.

"Jesus. Not now." Kal shook his lowered head and groaned.

Cora giggled. "Go get him. He can stay with me at the house and come into the office with me tomorrow. Freddie's there. Between the two of us, Sam will be fine."

Kal hesitated. "He's a big pain in the ass."

"You mean like his owner who's standing here arguing while the lights are turning on in some of the rooms and no doubt the switchboard is getting calls."

"Yeah, like that. Okay." Kal went to reopen the motel room and let Sam free. Cora had to giggle when the dog's nose rammed into Kal's butt, sharing his happiness for being allowed to come.

The trip to the airport went too fast and Kal seemed reluctant to get into mushy goodbyes once there. He looked deep into her eyes, kissed her nose, and walked away, no words spoken. Though she waited until she lost sight of him, he never looked back. She did see his fingers by his leg wiggle a wave, and she had to laugh. The bastard knew she hadn't left.

Cora and Sam returned to her house and pulled into the dark driveway. Curled on her doorstep, they found a little white bundle, waiting for her mistress. "How did you escape again, you little monkey?" The puppy wriggled so hard, her crying whimpers of joy overcame any animosity Cora might have felt.

"What's with you two furballs?" Sam's breathing all over the tiny puppy didn't seem to bother it. It wasn't until Cora lifted it to her cheek that the baby whined her delight at being reunited with the one person who belonged in her very small world.

In a short while, she had both her visitors on her bed with her, and they all cuddled close in the dark. Both Sam and the little one licked her face when the unexpected tears appeared, and both lulled her to sleep once their gentle support eased her suffering.

Chapter
Forty-two

Forced to take one of the connecting flights that had space, Kal stepped onto the plane. He was pleasantly surprised when the flight attendant led him to the business-class section, whispering that they'd had a cancellation and his name was chosen to fill the empty seat.

Settling down, he closed his eyes and would have drifted off but for the wailing coming from behind the separating curtain. It sounded like a child having difficulties, and his heart went out for the poor baby. He'd heard stories from co-workers of being on flights with their own children and the hellish times they'd had trying to control a screamer.

Tuning out the problem, he drifted off and was awakened by the air hostess. Her expression appeared rattled, and he sensed not only annoyance but disgust.

"What's wrong?"

"I'm sorry, sir. I know you're an FBI agent with a badge, and I hoped if you could flash it and speak to the passenger in 45C, you might be able to calm the man. He's out of control and scaring the other passengers."

"Okay. What's his problem?" Kal stood.

"It's the crying baby. The flight is pretty much full. I offered him your old seat but it's close to his own and won't make a difference. He's furious about the noise and wants us to throw the baby off the plane."

Kal stopped to face her. "Seriously?"

"He's lost all reason. The other passengers are afraid of him, and they won't settle. The woman sitting next to him refuses to take her seat. It's a nightmare."

Kal started forward and heard the male voice screaming almost as loud as the now hysterical baby. The mother's pitiful explanations were drowned out in the male's foul cussing. "She's only two months old and colicky. Her tummy is upset; she's thrown up every bit of milk I try to feed her."

"I don't give a fuck what's wrong with her. I paid a lot of money for this flight and all I ask is to be able to fucking sleep. That's all I want. To fucking close my eyes and not have to listen to the buzz-kill from your screaming brat."

By now Kal had approached the seat where the male's performance had gotten out of hand. He stepped close and when the asshole rudely glared at him, Kal's fist shot out, connecting with the bitcher's face. Silence followed and it was a few seconds before the voices nearby began laughing and congratulating Kal on handling the situation appropriately.

Out cold, the bleating bastard had his wish, and the rest of the folks totally agreed when Kal said, "Oops. I think I accidentally fell against this poor man and knocked him out."

The hostess nodded, her face wreathed in smiles. "Thank you, Agent Hunter. I saw it with my own eyes. It's so easy to trip over things on a plane. Thank you."

Kal grinned and looked over at the frazzled mother whose baby's cries grew louder. "Would you like me to hold the little one for a few minutes and give you a rest? I promise to be gentle."

"You want to hold her?"

"Sure. Maybe she just needs to hear a male voice that isn't screaming at her."

Almost comically happy to share her responsibility with an officer of the law who'd stepped up and taken control, she lifted the frantic child, blanket falling all around, and shoved her at Kal.

He took the tiny baby, rewrapped it, and snuggled her on his shoulder. Then he murmured low, gentle phrases, mostly humming the last song he'd heard Cora sing. He moved one way up the aisle and then back again while the baby's wails weakened to cries and then occasional sobs that eased off. He sensed she liked his shoulder against her poor tummy as if the pressure eased her discomfort. He patted her back gently and grinned when she burped. Poor little doll was in pain.

A few more trips back and forth up the aisle and one of the women close to her mother's seat whispered with a smile, "You've put her to sleep – not quite in the same way as you did with The Mouth."

Kal smiled and carefully handed the baby back to her young mother. "Her tummy was full of gas. Poor baby, sometimes a different kind of milk will help, that's what I heard from some of the women in the office. Worth a try if she stays upset with what you're feeding her."

"Thank you, officer. We all want to thank you for what you did earlier."

"You're all welcome."

Kal went back to his seat and hoped there wouldn't be any future repercussions over his manner of taking care of business.

He eventually arrived in the early hours of the morning, and other than a thank you from the pilot, again from the hostess, and a wave from the two cops called on board to look after the chastened troublemaker, all went smooth. He headed straight to the hospital only to find his mother had discharged herself late the night before and would be found at her apartment.

By the time he arrived there after fighting morning traffic and stopping to pick up some breakfast food for them both, he was letting himself in with his own key.

As if expecting him, his mom had made herself comfy in the soft blue leather Lazy Boy chair he'd given her last Christmas. Wearing a housecoat and covered with a fuzzy quilt, she seemed very relaxed. A smile touched her lips, and in her hand, she clutched a folded piece of paper.

Chapter
Forty-three

"Kal." She woke with a soft smile, her hand reaching for him. He leaned in and kissed her forehead, smiling in the special way he always did with her.

"Hi, lady. I heard you've been a naughty girl. The hospital said you discharged yourself last night. Why would you do that?"

"Because I don't believe it was a real heart attack. I think it was more the excitement from this letter."

Curious, knowing his mom to be a very sensitive individual, his confusion must have shown on his face. "First, I'll serve us the breakfast I picked up, and while we're eating, you can tell me what happened from the beginning."

His mom nodded happily and carefully placed the page in her pocket, fingering it like she'd just found a million dollars. Intrigued, he purposely didn't comment, and instead watched her walking in front of him. Steady as usual, she headed for the table.

Soon, they were settled in the area off the kitchen where he could see some demolition had taken place with the old rug missing and bare floorboard obvious.

He set out his purchases, the muffins she favored, and the fruit salads with yogurt. By the time he had everything to his liking, and they were ready to partake, he asked the question, "You're getting new flooring?"

Excitement filled her eyes. "Yes. Thank God I decided to do so."

Not understanding, Kal added, "I've been after you to upgrade this old place for some time now. Things haven't changed around here since Dad was alive."

"I know. I've been remiss, too crotchety to change my ways. Lately, age has caught up with me, and I realized I've just been letting life pass me by. I decided I needed a change of scenery and figured if I wanted to sell this place, it needed to be fixed up. When the men who were laying the new flooring came in to take out the old carpeting and tiles, they were forced to move that big old china cabinet your father's family gave us when we got married." She put down her mug and took the paper out of her pocket. Laying it beside her on the table, caressing the object as if it were alive and could feel her tenderness, she cleared her throat and continued.

"They found this stuck behind it. When I read it, I passed out and that's when they called the ambulance to take me to the hospital. Go ahead, you can read it too. I promise I won't call an ambulance if you have the same reaction."

"What is it?" He opened the page and saw what looked like a row of items with writing at the bottom.

"I believe your father wrote a series of reasons to help him take his own life."

His eyes flew to her face. "Excuse me? He did what?" Stunned, he followed her pointing finger and began reading out loud... until his voice broke.

My kid is the most important issue in this whole rotten mess.

Kal needs a healthy mom, a normal life.

Abby is weak and couldn't deal with a protracted death, fighting bone cancer... especially mine. It would destroy her. She's too sweet and gentle to watch someone she loves suffer.

I want every minute with them to be bright and not filled with my sickness.

I want her to be safe and find happiness, move on, and love again.

I want to be a man.

Lord help me, Abby couldn't handle watching me in pain day after day. She's been protected all her life and might succumb to drugs or booze, maybe both. I'll sell the car, take out my life insurance to pay off the apartment, and leave them in the best financial shape I can. A man does what a man has to do for the family he desperately loves...

The writing stopped there, and Kal felt the hit to his chest like the time he'd been tackled playing football by a bully twice his size. Breathing became painful. He had to inhale slowly.

With tears streaming, Abby reached out to take his hand. "I understand exactly how you feel, Kal. One minute he was there and the next he was gone. No goodbyes, no reasons for taking the bottle of pills, no hints of sickness. He'd protected us from all of that. And I hated him for doing it."

"I know." His voice broke. "I did too." Kal looked at his mother's streaming eyes, and his own flooded. "And you. I never forgave you for making his life so horrible he'd rather die than live with us. I'm embarrassed that I blamed you. I was a stupid kid."

"Since the day of the funeral, you've never called me Mom. I don't mind the nickname, Lady, but I've always known why you stopped, and it broke my heart. No matter how I tried to be the best mother possible, it didn't make any difference."

"God, I'm horrible. You didn't deserve a brat like me." He took her hands. "I'm so sorry, Mom." He leaned in and kissed her cheek. "His death mixed me up more than I ever knew. I thought I wasn't a good enough son for him to fight to stay with us... that his death was my fault somehow."

"See... I thought the same. I'd tried to be a good wife, but I'd been spoiled as a child, and he knew it. Your grandparents were well off and gave us kids everything. I was their youngest, the baby, and they made me think life owed me everything I wanted. Jack kept it up, spoiling me, handling me like a glass object too precious to take any hits. I let him down."

"No. Neither of us did anything wrong. He just did what he felt to be the best for his family. He thought we would forget and forgive and move on. He loved us both enough to want that for us."

Abby listened to his words and nodded. "When I first read the letter, all I saw were the words of love he had for me. It was like the chains were released and I was free from all the pain and remorse. Oh, Kal. I want to move on and start living my life or what's left of it."

"Lady, I have just the place I think you'd love."

Abby laughed at his wink and clapped her hands. "Tell me."

And he did. By the time he'd finished describing New Orleans, the balconied homes filled with trailing vines and colorful flowers, the warmth in the air, and the hearts of the friendly folks, he had her totally convinced.

"I'm going to get the men to move quicker on this renovation. I can't wait to meet your girl. I bet she calls her mother Mom."

"Amongst other things."

Abby laughed. "Lady suits me just fine."

Chapter
Forty-four

Cora slept a lot better than she'd expected to, probably the warmth of the animals in bed with her helped. In the morning, she quickly grabbed her phone to find a wonderful message from Kal. His mother was already home and feeling a lot better. It hadn't been a heart attack after all. He had good news to share and he missed her like crazy.

Rereading his words a few more times, she let the loving emotions wash over her. "Hey Sam, Kal says to give your floppy ear a pet from him." She reached over to wriggle Sam's ear and watched the dog behave sillier than she'd ever known him to be, puppylike and cuter than hell. *It must be his happy zone and Kal knows it.*

The zing from her phone meant another Breaking News item had hit the inbox. Scanning the various channels she checked each day, one of the happier items caught her interest and made her laugh. A warm feeling of gladness swept over her. Kal was catching the early plane back this morning and would be with her before nightfall.

Refreshed from a good night's sleep and happier than she'd been in a long time, she played with the lovable puppy and tried to come up with a name for her. Nothing seemed to suit the little monster, so she gave up. Then she rubbed Sam's belly until he groaned with pleasure before hitting the shower. With a happy step to her walk, she finished taking care of her chores at the house, dropped the runaway off at Mona's, and headed to the office.

Larry had been catching up with Freddie, waiting for her in her office. "Hey Toots, you look different."

"What do you mean, different?"

"You're smiling."

She lifted her middle finger and growled, "Bite me."

"Now, there's my girl. Kal contact you about his plane trip?"

Not sure where Larry was headed with this comment, Cora looked at Freddie and saw him trying to hide a grin. Before she could say anything, Larry held out a newspaper and there on the front page was a man walking a baby up the aisle of a plane filled with smiling people. Well except for one guy slumped in his seat, looking as if he'd passed out.

Cora laughed. "I already saw the article earlier.

Kal seems to have made a hit with the mother if that's her smiling up at him. He put her baby to sleep and gave the passengers a reprieve from the noise."

"Did you read the part about how he helped the air hostess deal with the problem complainer?"

"No. Where."

Freddie pointed at the smaller item further down. "Seems the guy was being an asshole and they called on Kal to step in. He fixed it with no fuss at all."

Cora read the short piece and laughed out loud by the time she'd come to the end. "They called him their angel. He'd hate that."

"Yeah, I know." Freddie cracked up. "Serves him right for leaving his comfort zone and helping that poor mom."

Now Cora showed her confusion. "What do you mean, comfort zone?"

"Kal has OCD, you know that, right? Sometimes it's so bad he won't touch anything, especially people. Getting Sam has helped him get over it somewhat, but he normally shies away from strangers."

"So, for him to take a crying baby was a big deal."

"Sure, of course. He's overcome a lot more since he's been here with you. It's been a real eye-opener watching him change."

Larry had listened and finally spoke up. "Maybe it's the place. New Orleans has a kind of magical vibe that works on some folks."

Cora and Freddie stared at the man in charge. Neither spoke and so Larry continued. "Maybe he should get a job at the Orleans's bureau and move here for good so the healing can continue. They'd snatch him up in a heartbeat."

When Freddie and Cora turned to look at each other and then back to Larry, their faces tried to contain their derision but failed. He waved their expressions away and added, "Just sayin'. Let's get to work. Where are we on finding our friend, Robbie?"

They spent the rest of the morning filling in the paperwork and trailing known lawbreakers for addresses. Once they had a shortlist of the smaller fries in the city, people who'd broken the law and were still walking the streets, Cora, Freddie, and Sam went to find them to give them the warning that they might be on a killer's hit list.

Screaming along the streets of the city, hitting the downtown area where the colorful trollies were quite a hit with the tourists, they soon found themselves in the darker sections. Here the devastation from Hurricane Katrina was still being felt today. Pulling up to what looked like a rundown apartment building on Warrington Drive, Cora parked the jeep.

Once the vehicle stopped, she got a kick out of the relief Freddie didn't hide. She watched as he let go of the bar he'd clung to by the window.

"The woman who owns this place, Sara Gleason, has quite a story." Cora's voice held muted fury. "She controls a lot of the working girls, and she's as mean as sin. Sends her girls out on the streets every night and works them hard every day. Recruits them young and once she has them in her clutches, they don't get free from her or the drugs she feeds them to keep them coming back."

"And she's still operating because…?"

"Because no one is willing to be a witness against her. We've tried, had it all set up earlier this year, and our witness fell to her death."

"Excuse me? Are you talking literally?"

"Yes. We were forced to claim it as a Hit and Run, but I suspect it was murder. A vehicle ran her over, and she ended up in a heap on the road. From the way the accident happened, we believe she was pushed. Funny thing, none of the other girls at Sara's will stand up to her now."

"Jesus. It takes all kinds, doesn't it?"

"No kidding. Come on Sam. Let's scare the shit out of Sara. It'll make my day."

With Sam close by Cora's side, they approached the messy house, yard full of junk, dirt, and weeds where grass should be growing, and broken pickets on a collapsing fence that hadn't seen paint in eons.

Before she had a chance to ring the doorbell, a fat, sloppy woman dressed in a well-washed, torn, satin housecoat, coffee stains, and who knows what else decorating the front, opened the screen door and came out on the step to block their way.

Her face might have been pretty at one time, but the bloated, pale skin had long ago lost any attractiveness. Puffy eyes, blotchy lined skin, and cracked lips indicated a woman who didn't care for her health, or her looks, just the stream of cats that showed up in every window and were seen around the yard, keeping their distance.

Sam had a way of terrorizing animals smaller than him, and today he meant business... at least his low snarls gave every indication of it.

"I'm honored, Officer Taylor. I haven't done anything to warrant a personal call from an elite cop like yourself, so why are you here?"

"Cut the crap, Sara. When are you going to clean up this mess? Your neighbors must be sick of your cats, and all the shit lying around."

"They don't complain. Or have they?" Sara's cold eyes narrowed, and she crossed her arms. "I keep to myself, mind my own business."

"Yeah, well it's your business we're here to discuss. Have you been recruiting any more youngsters? I told you what would happen if I find out you're up to your old tricks."

The old hag made a sound of disgust. "Trust me, I haven't pulled any tricks in a long time."

"That's probably the only thing you could say that I'd agree is likely true. Look, I'm here to warn you about a killer on the loose. He's targeting people like you who like to hurt others."

Sara spit, and the globby mess came close to landing on Cora's shoe. "S'at right?"

Disgusted, Cora managed to stand her ground. "I'm hoping by me coming here today, he'll pick up on your address and pay you a visit."

Maddened by Cora's innuendo, Sara lunged, her long uncut nails held like weapons only to meet with Sam's snarls of warning and Freddie's hand reaching for his weapon.

"I wish you would, Sara. Attack me. It would give me all the reason I need to defend myself, and I would love nothing better than to put a bullet right between those beady little eyes of yours."

"Trust me bitch, backatcha."

Cora turned her back to the scum lady and headed for the jeep, Freddie beside her. They heard Sam growl at one of the bigger cats who'd dared to come too close and watched as Sara frantically ran to the sidewalk to save her pet.

"Sam, come."

The dog turned to her and seeing her hand signal, he obeyed.

"Why didn't you let him have a go at that mangy thing?"

"Because, in a lot of cases, those mean cats are feral, and they fight dirty. Sam might get injured, and it wouldn't have been worth it."

"Oh, right. I get it. Why take the chance of him being scratched? Yet I've never wished more for anyone to make a move so I could have arrested her. She's vile."

"I know. But one day, she'll get hers. We'll keep working on it. I won't give up until that scum is behind bars."

"How many girls do you think she has working for her?"

"Most of them are women now, though she's always on the lookout for younger hookers. She promises them protection for a cut of their take, and she has a couple of sons loyal to her who are in charge of the street business."

Cora looked over to see Freddie still visibly upset over what he'd just witnessed. "Look, bro. We do the best we can. Sometimes we win and it's a good day. Often, we lose. But we don't stop trying. You can rest assured, one day I'll have her ass behind bars, her and her two brats, and we'll be rid of the menace."

"Until another one steps in to fill the void."

"Stop being so dismal. It is what it is. You lose some. You win some."

"Guess Kal is right. I'm a better agent for being in the office. This realty stuff is a terrible downer."

Cora laughed and headed to the next address. "You'll be better at your job for having some street experience. Stick with me, dude. You haven't seen anything yet."

Chapter Forty-five

Kal's plane landed in the dark of the night and this time he was able to catch a few winks while in the air. He couldn't wait to tell Cora about his trip and what he'd found out about his dad.

He still had trouble believing how his father's message appeared from the past. It's as if Kal's questioning his feelings lately had somehow mysteriously compelled the universe to answer the way it did. Not that he understood all that karma baloney, but it was mighty strange how the answers he'd been searching for lately suddenly appeared at the right time.

As soon as he came through the arrivals gate, he saw her, standing patiently, waiting for him to appear. Once he did, she waved, her fluffy hair a halo for her pretty eyes and smiles of welcome. Without hesitation, he swung her into his arms.

Lifting her body in the air, snuggling his face

in her warm neck, he sniffed her flowered scent and thrills ran through his rioting blood. God, she was as beautiful as he'd envisioned during his trip home.

"I can't wait to tell you about what happened."

"Goody. I can't wait to hear all about it... and about the female you had in your arms. And don't think of denying it. There's proof in the national paper."

Chapter
Forty-six

Though he'd left Cora hours earlier, Freddie still walked two feet off the ground. One day on the streets with that woman and she'd brought police work alive for him. Looking through her eyes, he'd seen city life more clearly than ever before.

There were so many poor, needy folks, good folks, who stared down futureless tunnels as if they had no chance in life, so what the hell were they battling for? Some thought wrongly that by breaking the law, it gave them the slight edge they needed to leave the slums and be somebody.

Little did they know, with cops out there doing the good work, protecting the others who didn't cut corners, many of the cheaters ended up paying the price for those weak choices.

He unlocked the door to his motel room, entered, and put his gun in the night-table drawer. Most often, he never even bothered to carry it with him. Today, Cora had insisted. Now he knew why.

It was a day he'd never forget. Made him glad he'd become a law officer, even if he'd chosen the FBI rather than being a city cop following in his father's footsteps.

No one in his family believed he'd amount to anything other than a techie and a gay techie at that. Showing them all he had as much grit and staying power as his brothers tickled his fancy. Knowing he liked girls not men was another thing he'd kept to himself out of sheer cussedness because of their attitudes.

Maybe he had some effeminate ways about him, he'd played that up as a kid and even as a younger man to get the laughs. Foolishly, the habit had stuck as a way to cover his shyness. But now, as a grownup, an FBI agent, he'd erected a chip on his shoulder that glowed neon – *you have no right to judge me, so fuck you. Think what you want.*

He'd picked up some Chinese food on his way home, knowing that tonight he'd be on his own. No doubt, Kal would be staying with Cora again. He'd seen the way those two looked at each other. Anyone with eyes and a heart could tell they were meant to be together. The guy deserved to be happy. Freddie felt that deeply.

After Shawn had retired, the others warned him that Kal would be a pain in the ass to work with. That he'd miss his old partner and wouldn't take kindly to anyone in his place. Freddie had gathered from the many stories the rest of the folks at the bureau shared that the two had worked together closely, and Kal had seen Shawn through both his divorces, making allowances for the man who made everyone laugh.

Though Kal had been standoffish as far as getting personal, Freddie had found him to be honest, kind, and he had no trouble understanding that Freddie's best role would be with the technical side so important in today's law enforcement. He'd never stepped over the line in any way, and Freddie had learned to trust the man. So much so that he'd come to idolize him as someone to live up to.

When frantic knocking at his door startled him, his first stunned reaction made him jump. Careful after being coached by Cora, he pulled his gun, stuck it in the back of his belt, and went to unlatch the door. What the hell? It was past midnight. No way Kal had arrived yet. His plane wasn't even due in for ten minutes.

Freddie left the chain on, looked out into the night, and saw a thin girl with a hood up over her hair. Her body was bent over, her arms curled around herself as if she were holding things together.

The harsh voice that spoke surprised him coming from such a small creature. "You work with Detective Taylor?"

Freddie looked behind her and to each side, making sure she'd come alone. "Yeah. I was with her today. What's wrong?" He unlatched the door to open it wider.

She pushed in and hid behind the door, getting out of sight as soon as possible. "Close the door. I don't want anyone seeing me here."

He did as she asked and locked it once again before stepping back to give her space. "I'm Special Agent Fred Falkner. How can I help you?"

"I-I work for Sara Gleason. The others at the house told me that you and Detective Taylor came to visit her today, and how Sara reacted afterward. She's scared of the cop."

"She's got good reason to be afraid of Cora. I've never met anyone who cares as much about what that insane cat-lover is getting away with. Cora wants to put her away for good."

"I think I can help, but I don't want to end up like Val."

"Val?"

"Yeah. Val Wheeler. She agreed to be a witness against Sara and her boys and ended up dead for her trouble. You've got to promise me witness protection or something like that... or I can't... won't talk."

Freddie had no idea how to handle the trembling, frightened girl, but he knew how he'd want someone to treat him, so he just did what he thought best. "What's your name, ma'am?"

She stared at him as if he'd stepped in a pile of shit. Her expression changed when she recognized his sincerity. "My name? Is that important?"

"I don't know what to call you, and ma'am somehow rings your bell, so maybe it's best if you give me a hint of what name you'd like me to use."

As if she understood, the shivering bundle of nerves spoke low. "You can call me Florence. It's my – my real name."

"Come and sit down, Florence. You're shaking." Freddie closed the window curtains and pulled out the chair at the small table that stood nearby. Then he replaced his gun in the night table. He didn't want to spook the young girl whose garish face plastered with too much makeup was barely keeping it together. He watched her sit and try to cover her thighs with a skirt that barely covered her girlie parts.

"Here. I have lots of takeout Chinese food. There's a microwave. I can warm it up for you. Then you can tell me what you know, and I'll promise it's off the record until you decide you can trust me. Deal?"

"Okay. I'm just terrified someone saw me come here."

"Were you being followed?"

"I don't think so, but Sara's sons watch us all the time. I got a – a John to let me off here rather than drive me back to the main street. I whipped down the alley, cut through a hotel lobby, snuck around the back, and waited. After ten minutes I came here."

"Good girl. You were careful. That's like a pro."

"I am a Pro."

Freddie stopped dead and turned to her. "I didn't mean like that. I'm sorry. Look, eat up and tell me why you came to see me." He put a carton of food in front of the girl, but she ignored it. Instead, she began to talk.

Hands clutching at the sweater she wore to hide the nakedness her black halter didn't cover; she started her story. "Val was my friend. She was the only one who treated me well. She cared about me. When she died, I was devastated. Sara could give a shit – other than she'd lost a worker. But for me, it was terrible. I lost my best friend."

"I'm sorry. It must have hurt."

"You'll never know. I tried talking her out of coming forward and talking with the cops, but she said she had to. It was the right thing to do. She'd seen the boys beat on one of the older girls who'd kept back some money. They almost killed her, and it pissed Val off. That, and the fact that they'd picked up a kid to work for them who can't be more than fifteen. Got her hooked on their shit drugs and now had one more bankroll to live off of. It's disgusting."

"Fifteen? Jesus."

"I have more. But I won't say another thing until that Cora person comes and tells me she'll take care of me personally. I don't want to die like Val."

"I'll call her right now. She'll come. Relax. Eat.

We'll talk about the weather, whatever. Just give her time."

Freddie picked up his phone and called the number. "Sorry to bother you guys, Cora, but this can't wait. One of Sara's girls just came to visit me at the motel. She needs to see you."

Freddie hung up the phone and turned to Florence, who sat waiting for his reaction. "She's on her way."

Chapter
Forty-seven

Cora put her phone back in her pocket and turned to Kal. He was greeting Sam who'd waited in the jeep at the airport.

"It's Freddie. He needs me to come to his motel room."

"Hey, tell him to get his own girl."

"Very funny. Seems he has a girl there already. One who wants to give evidence in one of the cases he saw with me today. I'll tell you all about it on the way over."

While she drove like the Indie driver she most often copied, she gave Kal the particulars of their house call to Sara's earlier.

Though he held on as usual, he listened as she spoke and shook his head with disgust at her mind pictures. "That woman sounds like a real winner. I hope this girl Freddie met has enough to put her away for good."

In a short time, they knocked on Freddie's door, and after checking they weren't followed, he let them in. "Cora, Kal, this is Florence Dayton. She was a friend of Val Wheeler, the—"

"The girl who was the hit and run case we couldn't solve. The one who came forward to put slimy Sara and her boys away. The one we didn't protect well enough, and they got to her." Cora's face wore an expression of sorrow mixed with anger. She moved into the room, making way for Kal to follow her. Stepping closer to Florence, she crouched down by her side. "I'm so sorry for your loss, sweetheart, but I'm still pissed that we let her down like that. She'd promised to stay at the hotel we'd booked her into, and we took her at her word. I should have known better. She left."

"I know. They got to her through me. I hadn't seen or heard from her for a few days. I didn't know she'd already gone to the cops and was worried sick about her. They said she was at some hotel with a customer and gave me the number. Said I should call and see if she was okay. They even gave me a couple hours off work so we could have time together. The so-called accident happened when she was on her way to our meeting place. I was devastated."

"Jesus. Look Florence, it's not your fault. You didn't know they would kill her. I'd do anything to put that ugly bitch, Sara, away for the lives she's ruined."

"Me too. Can you put her away with this?" Florence pulled out her phone, laid it on the table, and played a message. It clearly had Sara's voice congratulating one of her son's about following the instructions she'd given him to get rid of Val. Then another male voice laughed and said that her idea of pushing Val in front of a moving car that his brother drove had worked perfectly. They were well rid of the menace and it would keep the others in line if they knew what was good for them. Then Sara ended the discussion saying, "Any other bitch tries to mess with me, and I'll kill her with my own bare hands like I've had to do before." Florence, tears falling, shut off the tape, and pulled back as if it burnt her hand.

Cora sank on the nearest bed and stared at the crying girl. "Where did you get that?"

Kal handed the blonde hooker a box of tissues he'd gotten from the bathroom and stood back.

Grateful, Florence wiped her eyes and blew her nose. "I'd decided to go to Sara and ask why Val hadn't shown up to meet me. I was worried and hoped they'd know where she was. When I overheard them talking about Val, I opened my phone to record them. They'd kill me if they ever found out I did this." Val started crying again, harder this time, making her words difficult to hear. "It was murder. I couldn't sleep or eat, thinking about it. When – when one of the girls told me you'd come to see Sara today, and about her reaction, I decided to make a move."

"Reaction? What reaction?"

Calmer, Florence's overly made-up eyes widened as she answered with a sense of delight. "Sara's terrified of you. I mean shit-faced terrified. They say you've been hunting her for a long time and getting too close for comfort. Sara doesn't like it. But I do. I can't think of anything more fitting than to work with you to have her arrested."

Cora leaned over and hugged the startled girl. "Honey, you have no idea of what you've just done for me. I'm so happy, I could cry too."

"So, you'll do it. Take her down."

"Nothing would give me more pleasure."

"Will you tell me what happens? I need to know her expression when you tell her I'm the one who's kicking her ass. Me and Val."

"I promise." Cora gave the girl a side hug. "You're good people, Florence. Val would be proud of you."

"Will you be able to keep her and her boys behind bars? Should I be in witness protection?"

"With that tape, I can guarantee she'll not get free again."

Cora became serious and asked a lot more questions. By the time they had all the information she needed about the goings on at the house and where the boys would likely be at this time of the night, poor Florence was exhausted. Even Kal was slouching on the extra bed trying to overcome the jet lag from his travels.

He spruced up as soon as Cora had her plan in place and had called her regular team for backup. According to Florence, the boys would be at their usual bar watching the girls, collecting the money, and overall acting like the pimps they were.

Meanwhile, Sara would be at home with the girls working from the house, most likely surrounded by cats, eating junk food, and watching her shows.

Within the hour, Cora, Kal, and the uniforms were in front of the same house Freddie and she had visited earlier. Heart filled with joy for the coming arrest, she couldn't wait for the pleasure of seeing Sara's face.

The S.W.A.T. team knocked on the door and broke through when Sara refused them entry. Cora, gun pulled and ready, almost hoped that the stupid woman would try something so she could use it, but other than warding off attacking cats, the arrest went clean.

Sara's mottled face filled with fury, her eyes glaring her hatred, tried to attack Cora only to run into Kal's interference. Cora stepped close. "You're lucky Kal here is saving your life, you waste of skin. I'd like nothing better than to have to use my gun to protect myself."

"You got nuthin on me. I just live here. What else goes on isn't my business."

"Yeah... well, your girl Florence says the opposite. I believe her and especially the tape she has with you organizing Val's death. By the way, Florence wants you to know you messed with the wrong girl this time."

"She's a lying bitch."

"Yeah, yeah. Tell that to the judge." Cora watched two officers approach Kal to take Sara from the armlock he had her in. She followed them to the door to be sure they got Sara in the squad car.

She turned back to see Kal closing some of the furry marauders into the disgusting, dirty kitchen and brushing his hands against his jeans. "Crissakes, these felines are disgusting. I thought cats kept themselves clean."

"Look around at this mess. You figure any cats living here would care about personal hygiene?"

They stepped out of the way as the troops rounded up the few girls from their various rooms, snagged the johns trying to escape, and pushed at the still free cats that were underfoot.

The team leader approached, "Looks like we have everyone out now. Some of the boys are taking a second look, but I think we can close the place down for tonight at least. Thanks for calling us in on this, Cora. Me and my guys were tickled to help make this arrest."

"What's happening downtown?"

"No trouble. They picked up Sara's boys and a couple of their girls. Most scattered and will get a pass this time."

"Good. Thanks, Carl. I'll meet you at the station in a while to start the paperwork. These arrests have to go by the book. No errors."

"Got it. See you there."

Kal, waiting in the background, spoke, "I suppose you'll be busy the rest of the night?"

"Sorry, baby. This arrest is hugely important. Freddie will have Florence at the office by now, and I promised to join them as soon as I could and tell them all about what happened."

"No, no. Don't apologize. I'm thrilled for you. I'll hang around if you don't mind. Not saying I can keep my eyes open the whole time but being close to you is worth the pain of not having the night I'd planned."

Cora chuckled. "You and me both. Not a lot could keep me from following our plans... but this arrest – well it's something I've wanted for a long, long time."

Chapter
Forty-eight

The rest of the night and a good portion of the day ended up with both Kal and Cora hard at it in the office. Other than a short break for dinner, the hits just kept coming.

When Cora met up with Sara in the interview room, she loved seeing the other woman in chains, showing her fright. Knowing that Freddie had Florence with him behind the mirror, she purposely asked questions that would infuriate the vile woman and hopefully get her to lose her temper, speak of things she'd not willingly share.

Kal stood in the background, not believing that Cora was totally safe from the crazy bat they'd picked up. He'd argued his way in there by promising to say nothing.

Cora had laughed. "You just want to share in the fun. Okay, sure. Come in with me. If she comes at me though this time, let me handle her. I'd love to get my hands on the bitch and do some damage."

Surprisingly, Sara, calmer now, was hard to taunt. Keeping her mouth shut, she refused to answer any questions. The only time she showed any fight at all was when Cora hit her with the list of laws she'd broken. "We know about the fifteen-year-old you've messed with. That's child endangerment, along with trafficking of underage girls, drugs, prostitution and those are the least of your worries."

Sara kept a smug look on her face as she sneered at Cora. "My lawyer will have me out on bail by tomorrow."

Cora smiled, making sure the evil pleasure she felt was obvious. "Not this time, Sara. We also have you for the murder of Val Wheeler. No way is your fucking lawyer going to get you released... you or your boys. I know you'll miss your cats but take solace in knowing you'll be spending the rest of your life with two-legged ones in jail... the ones who take a hard line with women that mess with kids."

The malicious scream shook everyone who heard it... except Cora. She'd seen the breakdown in the beady eyes and relished it. Not expecting the reaction, Kal dove forward just in case but wasn't needed. Cora leaned in close, her eyes daring Sara to try something. For seconds everyone held their breath. When the old bat collapsed into sobs, Cora called for the officer to take her away. Then she turned to Kal and added, "She's just like most bullies when they hit a wall. No substance, just shit."

***

By the time the darkness had started falling again, and they'd finally caught up with the necessary paperwork to be sure they'd have a tight case for the prosecutor; Freddie reminded them of what night it was.

"I can't believe our killer hasn't struck yet. Tonight was the very night ten years ago when he hit the storekeeper at the convenience store, right?"

Larry stepped into their office area in time to add, "Looks like you spoke too soon, Freddie. I just got a call from Robbie Forrest's brother. He says Robbie's being held hostage and the kidnapper has him detained in the same place the last killing happened... you guessed it. Ten years ago."

"Jesus! When it rains, it pours, as my mom used to say." Kal stretched his back and rubbed his eyes.

Larry continued, "He insists that Cora and Kal deal with the hostage situation, anyone else comes near, and he'll kill Robbie."

Cora stood up and stretched too. "I'm surprised he hasn't killed him already. And I'm even more surprised that my give-a-shit-level is close to zero."

Larry patted her back like an older uncle. "Robbie's brother must have seen a few movies. He insisted he speak with Robbie or he'd take the call as a hoax. Robbie was crying, said the guy had a machete, and intended to use it. No doubt, it's our guy."

"Right. We never released the last type of weapon to the press. Looks like Larry's right." Cora looked at Kal and smiled, "Your call."

"No choice. But I go alone."

"Not gonna happen. He asked for both of us. It's the ending we should have had ten years ago."

Chapter
Forty-nine

Cora knew that Kal would have argued if she hadn't just walked out of the room, leaving him to follow... or not. She heard him running to catch up and turned, her finger pointing. "Not one more word. We do this together, or I do it alone. Up to you."

Kal held his hands up as if warding off the devil and said, "Larry's getting the team together to back us up as soon as they can. He promised to stay out of sight, but no way was he letting us go in alone. I figured you'd want to know."

"Hell, I was banking on him doing exactly that. He'd never leave one of his detectives hanging."

It was a quiet drive to where the killer waited for them. Sam seemed to recognize they were under stress. Other than laying his head on Cora's shoulder, rather than Kal's, as if to keep her from driving too crazy, he just slobbered and whined from time to time when she took the corner too fast.

Once they arrived at the convenience store to see it blackened, all the signs shut off except for the closed one that hung in the window, Kal followed Cora to the back of the jeep.

She took out the Kevlar vest for both herself and Kal and surprised him when she also took out one for the dog. Proudly, standing still while she put it on him, Sam looked at Kal with his mouth hanging open as if grinning his acceptance of being one of them.

Kal rubbed his ear exactly how he liked it and then took Cora in his arms. "Promise me to be careful. I can't lose you. I couldn't survive."

"A man of few words and all of them the ones that count. Okay, my turn. If you let that son of a bitch get close enough to hurt you, I'll shoot him first and then you for making me live through hell."

He chuckled and kissed her so deeply she had no doubt that he cared about her. "Your mother's really planning on moving here?"

"That's the latest."

"And you're coming with her?"

"Kinda stands to reason."

"Fine, let's get this over with so we can put a closed stamp on this fucking case and go home. I want to show you how happy that makes me feel."

Not waiting for him to reply, she headed toward the building, him following her closely, and stopped behind the fuel pumps so she could call out to the killer. "Hey, you in there. Kal and I are outside. Now what?"

"I knew you'd come for this low-life bastard who didn't deserve to take another breath. I never doubted it for a minute."

"Hell, we're not here to save his ass. We're here to get yours and put you away where you belong."

"Ain't gonna happen. Before the night is over, I'll be where I belong, and it won't be in a jail cell... but with the devil who's been riding my back since this mess started."

Cora heard Kal's moan and turned to see his expression filled with fear. Tears showed in his eyes, and he appeared... shattered. She began to shake. "What? Kal, what's wrong?"

"You were right all along. That's not the cold-case killer. He's my old partner, Shawn."

A punch to her face wouldn't have had near the shock his words gave her. "Are you sure?" She shook her head to clear it and then answered her own query. "Of course, you are. What do you want to do?"

Kal rolled his lips together and fell back on his butt. Sam approached as if he understood Kal had taken a hit big enough to take him down.

Cora sensed she would be in charge and so she tried to give Kal the time he needed to deal with this new turmoil. She turned back to the convenience store where Shawn waited. "Is

Robbie still alive?"

"Hell, no. He not only killed the girl you knew about, but he's done it before, more than once. I have the files at the hotel. When this is all over, you'll have everything you need to understand why this swine couldn't be allowed to live. Is Kal okay?"

"What do you think? He believed in you."

"Yeah, I know. He'll find out that I didn't retire with an inheritance from my grandmother. I used all of my savings to finance this expedition. And I'm not sorry. He knows about the army. How I felt about being a sniper for the government. Killing without mercy for the ones they wanted dead. Believing it was my duty. I was already heading for Hell when the old doc told me I had an inoperable brain tumor and only months to live."

Cora waited to see if Kal wanted to speak. When he didn't say anything, she tried to keep Shawn talking. "I get it. After the army, killing came easy to you."

"Not at first. Not until I shut off my conscience and did my job. I was good at it, won awards. They gave me medals for killing. And why not? Most of the creeps I hit had it coming. That's when I got the idea for this adventure."

"This adventure? You mean the ten-year-old cold-case file?"

"Yeah. Kal and I often cleaned up these cases, and when I found out that the real killer had died by his own hand years ago, I didn't add that to the file. Instead, I studied everything he'd done and decided I would re-enact his assignations but with one difference."

"You'd only kill those who deserved to die."

"Right. You got in the way. That shouldn't have happened. I'm sorry you had to suffer. You okay now?"

"Yeah. Thanks for the flowers."

"Is Kal going to talk to me?"

Cora looked over at her man and saw his head still bowed.

"Doesn't look like he has anything to say. You ready to come out now?"

"I guess. You ready to shoot me rather than make me suffer the pain and indignities of dying in jail?"

"Nope. You have to face the judge like everyone else who breaks the law."

"I'm facing the only judge that matters to me, sweetheart, and he refuses to say anything." The silence only lasted a few seconds before his voice called out again, "Sam. Come to Shawn."

The dog had recognized the voice but hadn't moved from beside Kal until he was called. Before they could grab for him, he ran toward the building where a man holding a rifle stepped into the light of the one sign that said closed.

He lifted the rifle and took aim at the dog, letting a round loose but purposely missing his target. Kal flew to his feet, his gun in his hand, his voice raw. "Don't Shawn. Please. I forgive you. Jesus man, don't kill Sam."

Cora saw the determination on the stranger's face as he pointed the rifle again. Her hand lifted with her gun, and she didn't hesitate. One shot and he dropped.

Chapter
Fifty

"You sure you're okay?" Cora snuggled beside Kal on the bed where she'd brought him after the hullabaloo died down.

"He was going to kill Sam." Kal reached out to stroke his companion not caring that the dog was beside him on the bed. "My best friend was willing to shoot Sam."

"Just to force us to shoot him. Shawn wanted to die, Kal. You know that. Facing his future, I don't blame him. And he wanted you to be the one to help him."

"Why couldn't he just do it for us? Why did he make us have to be the ones to take his life?"

"I don't know. Hell, maybe a shrink couldn't even tell you how his mind worked at the end. He was sick, on a lot of pills. From the coroner's initial investigation, he figures Shawn suffered terrible pain. Could be his mind wasn't clear."

"Maybe."

"All I know is he loved you. You were the one he came to in the end, the one he called for when he died. I'm so glad you went to him and forgave him. He deserved to die with you holding him."

Kal turned toward Cora, her hand held tightly in his. "This time you took the shot, didn't hesitate. I'm not sure I would have."

"And take the chance he might actually kill Sam to force our hand. Or hurt you. I couldn't bear it if I lost either one of you."

"Thanks for coming to his hotel room with me. I always knew Shawn to be sloppy to a fault, but this time he proved he had the ability to be neat and organized all along. Each immaculate file was sorted by date, and he'd even added his own comments as he'd closed them."

"I liked the way he'd made them personal to you, as if he'd thought of you as still being his partner."

"Yeah. That was his style. He'd made the whole procedure into a game where he became judge, and I was his jury. Each record, he described how he'd made the choice of who to kill and why."

"I saw your face as you read through them. You were with him every time. You would have chosen guilty for each victim. He didn't want you to ever suffer over his decisions, but rather to be relieved at his choices."

"He believed in the law, but in his own way. I guess the training they'd forced on him had stuck."

"I didn't know Shawn, but I respect him, Kal. I can't say I'll ever be able to think badly of the guy. Not when he brought us together again." Cora felt the tears hovering and had no intention of spoiling this moment. "Enough. Let's talk about something happy."

"You got it." Kal kissed her, and then he reached out to stroke the little white snuggler held close to Cora's body. "I can't believe she was waiting for us in the dark. Have you decided on a name for the fluff magnet yet?"

"Kinda thought Hurricane might suit her. She's like a storm that keeps on coming."

"Besides being ridiculous, it's too big a mouthful. How about Snowy?"

Cora scoffed. "That *is* ridiculous. Maybe Gunner?"

Kal roared just like Cora had hoped when she threw out the ridiculous name. "Okay, so maybe that's not gonna work. Your friend's last name was Bonaire. How about we call her Bonny. She's shown to be a true friend by coming back to me every time."

They both looked at the puppy when she lifted her head, opened her tiny mouth to grin, and finished with a sleepy whine.

Kal chuckled, his husky voice showing tiredness. "Very appropriate! She is a bonny lass, isn't she?" He yawned and forced his eyes back open. "I just have one request that needs an answer before I can sleep."

Cora leaned over to place a kiss on his cheek and then lay back down as if the energy it took to do even that was overwhelming. "Anything... I think."

"Could the torn sleeve on that wedding dress I saw you wearing the first day I got here be repaired? It's been a fantasy of mine to see you wearing it in a church, coming toward me up the aisle. I'm talking as soon as possible."

Cora laughed. "You know that dress isn't really my style."

"Baby, it suited you so well, I fell in love with you the first moment I saw you in it."

"Really? Fine, I'll take it to the dressmaker's tomorrow."

Afterword

Thank you so much for reading Book # 10 of the Undercover FBI Series – *Special Agent Hunter*

I loved working on this book, and I hope you enjoyed reading it too.

If you liked this story, I would ask you for a favor, please take a few minutes and leave an honest review. Authors enjoy hearing that readers like their stories, and hopefully, others will read your words and choose to buy the book because of your sentiments.

My website at http://mimibarbour.com now has all my books listed with links to the publisher to make it easy for you to return to where you bought the book and to find my other work.

While you're there, I'd really appreciate it if you would sign up for my newsletter so I can keep in touch. http://bit.ly/MimiBNewsletter. I only send out newsletters approximately twice a month. It's usually full of giveaways, contests, and freebies, along with my personal news. (You have my word that your address will never be shared.)

Hugs, Mimi

Special Agent Sophia

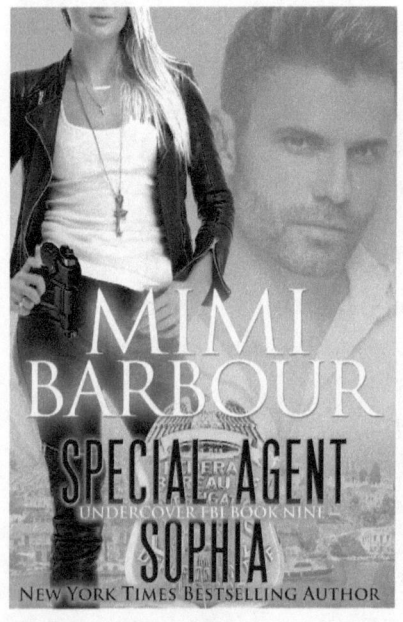

Undercover FBI Book #9

by
  Mimi Barbour
  NYT & USA Today Best-selling author

Sophia's mane of silver hair gives her the look of a mystical warrior, a female not of this world. Some colleagues defend her, others are jealous, most fear her, yet everyone respects her abilities. An ace sharpshooter, she's called on for the most difficult cases. Her uncanny ability to remain cool under duress makes her the perfect person to rescue the twins of the frantic governor whose rejected husband intends to make her suffer. The fact that they are whisked to Greece also works in her favor since she's spent most of her summers in Rhodes visiting family and can show up there without anyone becoming suspicious. Problems begin when a cocky hero hits on her in the marketplace. Why her?

Sam Reagan, owner, and CEO of The Reagan Group promises his sister he'll follow the FBI agent to the Greek island to ensure his niece and nephew are safely returned to her arms. Understanding his mission has to be covert because his former brother-in-law will recognize him if he steps out of his undercover role, he uses an alias and follows the gorgeous agent who's on the case. It's understood he stays in the background, gives assistance if needed... until he sees her. Then all bets are off. There's no way he'll leave her to deal with dangerous traffickers after she saves a teenager and whisks the poor girl away right under their noses.

Digging deeper, working together, they discover the consortium of criminals is more organized than they first believed. And the man running the operation is the same low-life loser who fathered the missing twins.

Praise:

"Special Agent Sophia is the ninth book in the Undercover FBI series and is a great romantic suspense story.
I love this series. The agents are always strong yet feminine and Sophia is no exception. She is sent to beautiful Greece to find children who were kidnapped by their father. The characters in this book are well depicted, likable, and realistic. The storyline is well crafted and has amazing descriptions of Greece and its surroundings and atmosphere. This book held my attention from start to finish with missing children, human trafficking, suspense, danger, and romance." ~ **Reviewed by Heather**

"What a good book! As usual, this author does not disappoint. Every book I've read written by her is very very good! I highly recommend this book if you like a little romance and lots of suspense. On to the next one!" ~ **Reviewed by Vernemo**

Special Agent Sophia - Chapter One

Special Agent Sophia Dunne stalked past two girls in the outer office and glared at them, saying without words that she found Maisie filing her nails an irritation; and Heather, who was giggling like a teenager on a personal phone call, an affront to what they should be doing in the FBI office.

When Suzi, one of the desk agents, followed, she found the two with their heads together, talking smack about the one person she wouldn't allow anyone to put down.

"What's up with you guys? Haven't you got any work to do?"

"Shit, you're as bad as the ballbreaker." Maisie threw a folder back into her desk drawer and slammed it with some heat. "Jesus! Can't a person file a cracked nail without getting the nasty eyeball around here?"

"Who had the guts to give you a nasty look?"

"Who else but your BFF."

"And me, I wasn't on the phone longer than a

few minutes, just organizing dinner plans with a new admirer on eHarmony. So, sue me! Sophia's got such a stick up her ass, I bet she hasn't had a man take her out in years."

Suzi didn't want to let them talk crap about her friend. Not today, not after what she just found out. It wasn't in her to listen to this garbage without feeling the rub. If they only knew Sophia for the person she was, they'd shut their yaps. But she knew when to keep her own council and would have walked out if they'd have stopped there.

The two, giggling like bad girls in a high school cluster, kept up the bullshit – mean and full of self-righteous justification – and it cracked her resolve.

"You guys are so full of shit you make fools of yourself every time you open your mouths. Sophia has more heart in her body than both of you doubled. Remember last week when Lisa in IT was staring at an eviction notice because she hadn't made the rent for two months. It goes without question when a mom worries about paying for her kid's asthma medication or paying rent, it's a no brainer. Then she found out some anonymous donor had paid her back payments and even covered this month's rent. Well, it sure as shit wasn't one of you hyenas who stepped up, was it?"

"Seriously? Sophia did that? How did she know Lisa needed help?"

"She overheard the landlord on the phone reaming Lisa out and threatening her with eviction."

"How did you find out?"

"I was there. A few minutes after the call, Sophia left. A little while later, I had to call her out for that shooting on Main Street, and I heard the man in the background saying it was a good thing Lisa had friends because he didn't really want to make her leave. But he had bills to pay too. I knew where she was then."

Heather slapped her hands on the desk as if frustrated, her expression full of self-recrimination. "That convinces me."

"She'd kill me if she ever found out I'd let the cat out, but it burns my butt listening to you two go on about her when I know she puts *her* goodness and *her* money where *your* mouth is. So stop with the bellyaching and help her when she asks. Otherwise, mind your own fucking business."

"Son of a bitch!" Maisie piped up, shaking her head. "She's the last person I suspected; figured it was the boss, Bruner." The heavyset bleached blonde leaned back in her chair. "Look, Suzi, we'd be happy to friend her but it's impossible to get past the shield she hides behind. And even harder after they sent her to that training program in Texas, what's it called again?"

"You mean the ALERRT – the Advanced Law Enforcement Rapid Response Training program?"

"Yeah, that's the one. It's like she struts around with a superior chip on her shoulder all the time.

And her hair freaks me out. How can someone so young have pure silver hair? Bloody stuff is natural too. I don't get it."

"You're crazy, you know that? Her hair's gorgeous and... she's fucking shy. If you talked to her once in a while rather than ignore the woman, you'd see that. And if your career meant that you were called out to every incident involving a hopped-up crazy with a gun, maybe you'd have your head in the job too. It can't be easy knowing your skills are used to kill someone."

Maisie added, "Yeah, but just remember, they're the bad guys who need to be stopped before they kill civilians. It's understandable who has to die. Plus, I've heard she opts to wound them almost every time. Come on... she's doing a necessary job."

"Okay, but you try going out there and put yourself on the line. See if you don't get a serious side."

Heather added, "And don't forget, she's one of the best we have in this state. Last week, she shot that asshole, Sopher, when he tried to hide behind a kid for heaven's sake. Who does that?"

Suzi began breathing easier knowing she'd turned the tide of their condemnation. Now they viewed her friend the way she'd always known Sophia to be. After all, if her silver-haired friend hadn't been on the spot when Suzi's own mom had shot up with the fentanyl-laced heroin, they'd have lost her. It was Sophia's grasp on the situation that saved the older woman. It was the night she'd come for dinner after numerous invitations. Then she'd excused herself right after Suzi's mom had gone out to meet up with a friend. She'd been the one who'd trailed her to a dark alley where she bought her drugs. And, she'd been there after her mom shot up.

If she'd have walked away, the injection would have killed her. But she'd called an ambulance and then hung around, making sure her mother stayed upright and conscious. When the ambulance showed up, she was able to tell them exactly what happened so they could administer the Naloxone that saved her life. They'd brought her mother back from the brink and Suzi felt a debt she'd never be able to repay.

How Sophia knew her mom was using, and she herself had missed it, still irked her, made her question her own abilities as an investigator. Sure, because of her injured leg, she worked mainly from the office, but she'd still been trained in Quantico like the rest of the agents.

The car accident that had her pinned in the driver's side for an hour before they'd found her caused not only her problems, but it was what led to her mom's later downfall. The opioids they'd given Suzi for her pain had sat in the medicine cabinet unused. Knowing how addictive they were had pretty-much stopped her from taking them. She'd lived with the agony until it became unbearable. She'd broken her resolve twice and resorted to the pills cut in half, welcoming the relief, and then pissed at herself for giving in.

It was her mother's back pain that led the older woman to go searching for some respite when she'd stumbled on the medication and had begun using it unknown to Suzi. That's the moment the devil had stared her mom in the face, and she'd succumbed. Suzi often wondered if she'd known how addictive they were. Nervous to know the answer, Suzi never asked.

Thanks to Sophia, today she was comfortable in a rehab facility that had convinced her to stay on in the position of a live-in therapist. Being a psychologist before she'd retired, her counseling skills were desperately needed for the folks who lived the same sickness she'd just overcome. Once she'd totally kicked her own habit, she could speak with the voice of one having gone through hell herself. After her back operation, it had all worked out.

It was one of those nightmares that eventually turned out to be the best thing that could have happened. And a year later, both Suzi and her mom thanked God for her friend's quick thinking and kindness.

***IF YOU'D LIKE TO CONTINUE READING THIS BOOK, YOU'LL FIND IT LISTED WITH AMAZON!

Retaliation - Book #1 - Her Sweet Revenge Series

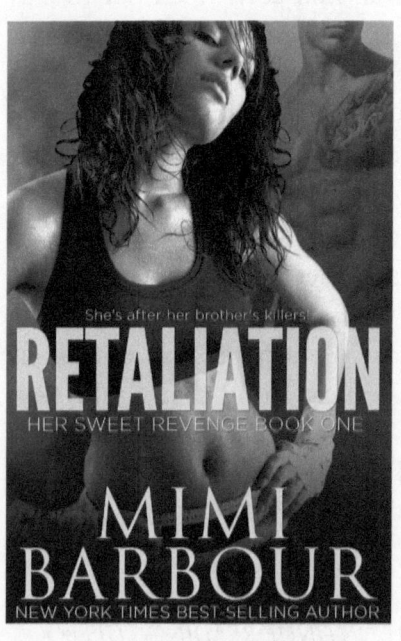

FREE on all major venues!

by
  Mimi Barbour
  NYT & USA Today Best-selling author

*** *Warning: This is a series that must be read in order!!*

A virgin librarian with hot-chick potential, the conflicts in her story won't let you put the book down. Be prepared for an all-nighter...

She watches the mob kill her twin and is too frozen with fear to stop them. How can she live with that cowardice eating away at her self-respect? Revenge claws at her sheltered existence until she can't breathe. Though she's naïve, she isn't stupid. When she finds a stash of loot in her brother's gym locker, she has the means.

Now all she needs is the guts to make every one of those low-life gang members pay.

People might think detectives are hard-assed cops with no home life, but Trace McGuire has a dying mom he loves fiercely. Already stressed over his personal problems, he takes a bullet for a virgin beauty hiding while mobsters shoot her brother.

This chick draws out every protective instinct he thought had disintegrated over years on the job and he becomes invested – in her hot body, her plans for retaliation and her fighting spirit.

Helpless, he watches her enter the seedy underworld that'll eat her alive.

Then he sees her fight.

And wonders if they'll survive her.

Praise:

"I am in love with this book and I'll be following the series for more! Mimi Barbour did an awesome job!" ~ *Reviewed by Birna Bjornsdottir*

"Trace – oh Trace how I love you! As soon as he appeared in the story I knew I would fall in love with him and I did! He was a really great character, independent, focused and not afraid to push the limits when needed. Together he and Cass were amazing!

I really cannot wait to read more from this author in the future and highly recommend this story! You will have a hard time putting it down once you have started!" ~ *Reviewed by Katie_83*

"Ms. Barbour has written a gripping story about one woman's quest for justice. She has deftly created marvelous characters that pull you into their story. This is a suspense-filled, full-bore non-

stop action ride that you will absolutely love."
~~Reviewed by Colorado Avid Reader

About the author - Mimi Barbour

MIMI BARBOUR: New York Times & USA Today Best-selling romance author has written nine series and over 45 books. She lives on the beautiful East coast of Vancouver Island and writes her books with tongue-in-cheek and a mad glint in her eye. The fans all agree that it's the fascinating characters she creates which makes her writing so entertaining and brings them back for more of her magic.

"The favorite part of my job is meeting the characters from each new book. Designing them the way I want and having them act however I think they should. It's thrilling, especially when most of my make-believe folks are so very interesting. They're fun and surprising, and in most cases, people I would love to interact with in reality."

Contact Me

Amazon author page: http://bit.ly/
MimiBarbourAmazon

My website: http://www.mimibarbour.com/

Or follow me on twitter: https://twitter.com/
MimiBarbour

Or on Facebook: Mimi Barbour Fan page

Please sign up for my fun Newsletter: http://bit.ly/
MimiBNewsletter

or

Write to me anytime. I love to hear from my
readers xo
mailto:mimibarbour66@gmail.com